SEARCHING

A PREQUEL to *THE STARLIGHT CHRONICLES*

C. S. Johnson

Print ISBN: 9780999672808

EBook ISBN: 9780999672815

For Sam. Finding you was no accident, and befriending you was a miracle.

This is also for Ryan, for your faithfulness to me. That was a miracle as well, but one, miraculously, that I was able to choose.

Finally, this is for Gummy Bear. Your momma said you would be a fan, so I write in the hope you will one day read this and smile.

To Get *Awakening* (A Christmas Episode of The *Starlight Chronicles*) as a bonus for picking up this book,

Or Download It At:
https://www.csjohnson.me/awakening

AUTHOR'S NOTE

Dear Reader,

Those of you who are familiar with my work know that there are rare exceptions when I write a letter at the beginning of the book rather than at that the end. In this book, I fully intend on making a further exception, having one at the beginning *and* one at the end. This is really only because I'm having a moment where I am "Magician's-Nephewing," which is my term for writing the book of a series that takes place before the series, and only doing so after the rest of the series is published. C. S. Lewis and his influence on my life strikes again, and I am more amused at how surprised I am at it than I am surprised at it.

I started writing *Slumbering* at the end of high school. It would take many rewrites and many years before I had the courage to share it, and even more to willingly promote it, and then to finish the series. Almost as a birthday gift to myself, or maybe more as an early 10-year-high-school-reunion gift, I finished the series with *Everlasting* in the early part of 2017.

But as the audio books and the graphic novel for *Slumbering* began, I felt a creeping feeling, one that I almost loathed to admit: The series was still not complete.

In rereading the books for their respective adaptations, I found that I had a lot to explain yet when it came to Starry Knight, and even more so, there were things she wanted to explain. So, if you are picking up this book, and it is the first book of the Starlight Chronicles you are reading, you might find several spoilers for further along down the way, and you might be better served in starting with *Slumbering* first.

5

I guess that's an easy enough way of saying, "Spoilers ahead," and "you've been warned."

Thus, my duty to you as author and entertainer is fulfilled, and it is now up to you, to choose your duty to your heart. I can assure you, either way, it's a good story, and whether you are new here or not, I hope you will stay on until the end. After all, the beginning has very little merit on its own if it goes nowhere, right?

Until We Meet Again,

C. S. Johnson

SEARCHING

A PREQUEL to *THE STARLIGHT CHRONICLES*

C. S. Johnson

THE STARLIGHT CHRONICLES

☼1☼
The Beginning I Want to Begin From

I was very young when I first learned the power of a broken heart.

Fortunately, or maybe unfortunately, it was not my own heart that taught me this truth. My heart, after all, was already broken.

And that's why I'm here, I thought wryly, glancing up from the all-too-familiar patient room floor at Apollo City Hospital.

Between the tarnished sense of sterility, its ash-colored tiles, and the dulled-white walls, I almost felt at home. In the last six years, I'd come here at least once every couple of months. Between all my visits, I had counted the cabinets along the wall countless times, even if I always forgot how many there actually were in the end.

That wasn't the only thing I'd forgotten, either. I frowned at the sudden, overwhelming scent of iodine.

How long have I been sitting here, to have forgotten that?

I hated that smell. It wasn't just unpleasant in itself; it also brought up a wide array of unpleasant memories.

"What is it, Raiya?"

Despite my discomfort, a small, reassuring smile was already on my lips as I looked over at my grandfather. Through the loose tresses of my coppery hair, I saw him watching me with a concerned look on his face.

9

My grandpa was a thin man, with a bushy, white beard and kind, ageless eyes. Every day since I'd finished elementary school, it seemed as though he was getting shorter as I was getting taller. As I gazed at him, taking in his plain clothes and his oversized coat, I thought how easy it would be for the average person to dismiss him, to see him as harmless and old, barely indistinguishable from any man walking in the street.

Grandpa would never be that to me. No—to me, he was my hero.

Grandpa was the one who brought me back to the United States after my parents died in a car crash in Norway when I was seven years old. After nearly dying in the crash myself, and losing what seemed to be my whole world at the time, he was the one who kept me going.

He was my hero then, and ever since, he had become a friend, a mentor, and a confidant.

"I'm fine, Grandpa Odd," I said, letting his dark chameleon eyes meet my own blue-violet ones. As I held his gaze, I felt a world of unspoken trust pass between us, and I saw his concern visibly lessen.

Of course, that still didn't stop him from asking the inevitable question.

He crossed his arms and leaned back against the faded medical poster on the wall behind him. "Do you want to talk about it? We have a few moments before Dr. Dinger comes in."

It was as if he knew I was desperate to hide the truth from him. But then, I supposed Grandpa already knew some of what happened. The school officials would have had to tell him *something* when they asked him to come for me.

My fingertips tightened against my cot, pressing into its smooth plastic and crumbling the overlying paper. Beneath the brown and white colors of my Rosemont Academy uniform, I felt the back of my legs tingle with alarm.

"If you tell me exactly what happened, I might be able to tell you what went wrong. We will need to figure it out."

I went still for a long moment—long enough to make it seem like I was thinking over his words. But I already *knew* what went wrong.

I'd broken my best friend's heart.

Grandpa sighed, seeming to step back. "Everything will be alright, Raiya. This is part of growing up."

"I'm just … still processing it all," I lied. "It doesn't help that I feel guilty."

"Guilt misapplied is an abuse of the heart."

"Well, I would know something about abusing my heart," I replied jokingly, glancing around the room. "After all these years coming to see Dr. Dinger."

Grandpa Odd smiled, knowing my humor was as much a way for me to protect myself as it was to reveal myself. "It is true that in the last couple of years since we've started to come and see him, you would know matters of the heart

11

inside and out. But the heart often has a mind of its own, and a realm all to itself."

Again, I said nothing. I knew what he said was true; Grandpa didn't have to remind me of that.

If there are any reminders I need, Reggie is the one offering the more important one today, I thought bitterly.

Reggie was the reminder that it was dangerous to let people get close to me.

Wasn't that the reason I was sitting in a hospital room in the first place, waiting for my practically on-call cardiologist to come and order another round of blood testing and chest x-rays after one of my full-blown, so-called panic attacks?

At least Dr. Dinger is a nice guy, I told myself.

Of course, that hardly made dealing with this stuff any easier.

"You cannot ignore the truth, Raiya," Grandpa said quietly. "You know the truth about who you are, and why you are here. It does not help hiding it, either."

I shot a quick glare at him before turning my attention to the window. Outside, it was a bright August summer day, perfect for northern Ohio. The cerulean sky and the shining sun reminded me all over again that school had just started.

Seventh grade was already going to be the worst year of my life, I thought.

"I know my destiny," I heard myself say, my voice steady even if my resolve was not.

"Then you know why you cannot run from the truth."

Exasperated, I held out my hands.

In the twinkling of an eye, my palms were overflowing with a bright violet light. It soared out from my heart, over my hands, and then burst across the room; it scattered like lightning, crinkling with power and light, both lovely and frightening. I held steady, letting my gaze follow the elegant, ragged lines of energy, watching each ray as it glimmered all the way down each stagnant end.

I marveled all over again at the power I held inside of me, the small things that distinguished me from being just a normal human being.

A rueful smirk curled onto my face; Grandpa wasn't the only one who was more than he seemed. After six years, I knew the truth, and there was no mistaking it.

I was a fallen Star, an *Astroneshama*, a Starlight Warrior and a defender of Earth. I was born in this realm to protect it, to correct my previous life's mistakes, and to die for a purpose that was both my own and the furthest thing from my own.

Grandpa had taught me about my origin, telling me who I was and where I came from, guiding my morality and affirming my dignity, all which in turn shed light on my ultimate destiny.

13

My Starlight power, innate and inseparable from myself, confirmed Grandpa's insight.

Every Star has power, and every Star has a wish. My power was among the most dangerous; inside of me, I could both heal and destroy, and the difference between the two came down to my own judgment.

My wish, I knew, was gone. But since there was nothing I could do about it, my power was the more pressing issue, and rightfully so.

If someone were to ask me about it, it would have been hard for me to explain. How do you really explain something like that to someone who can't see the truth of your experience? It had to be similar to explaining what color was to a blind person, or what music sounds like to a deaf person.

I just knew, deep down, with the truth penetrating into my whole being, what I could not ignore mattered, and it mattered more deeply than I could ever explain.

I *knew* that.

So the idea Grandpa thought I was being flippant about this, this situation I found myself in, was more than a little insulting.

I watched as he flinched at my power's outpouring, feeling more than a little self-righteous.

The spindles of my power blinked brightly, bringing me back from my wandering thoughts.

"I know I cannot run from it, Grandpa," I finally said, pushing the waves of my power around the room into a quick spiral, before my fingers stretched and I pulled it back into me once more. A rush of welcome warmth broke across my heart as the light dispersed inside of me and flickered away. "It's part of who I am."

"Your control is back, I see," Grandpa noted. "That's a good sign. Do you want to talk about what happened to that boy now?"

I blushed at Grandpa's soft rebuke. But I shook my head; I wouldn't tell him about Reggie. It was the least I could do for Reggie, anyway, since we would never be friends again.

Reggie had been my friend since my first day at Rosemont Academy, just over four years before.

Back then, Grandpa and I had recently moved in with my cousin, Rachel Cole, and her mother, my Aunt Letty, who was my father's ex sister-in-law, or something like that. I didn't care about how we were related; I was just relieved to have some semblance of a family again, even if it was not the one I longed for.

The first day of school was hard for me, especially in that expensive, uncomfortable Rosemont uniform; I remember it well, because as much as it helped me to blend in, it still made me feel like even more of an outsider. Rosemont was a proud and lovely school, sitting in a small, protected area near the heart of Apollo City. While Grandpa assured me that the school was a good place for me, I knew he had called in a few favors to get me in.

That was probably the only reason I relented in going at all.

Walking through the nearly empty halls on my first day, I allowed myself to have some hope. The building's strong columns and the high ceilings, slanted windows and open hallways, gave me a sense of curious wonder and somehow inspired courage. Looking back, I know that the school's atmosphere enchanted me; when you are seven years old, and you have no home of your own, you tend to think that you can easily find a new one if you try hard enough.

No one talked to me as I headed toward my classroom. I saw some teachers and a few other students, some of them very loudly chatting with their friends. I wondered at their ease, envious of their comfort. The first time I spoke myself, it was to correct my teacher when she called my name for attendance.

"It's Raiya," I insisted, probably sounding ruder than I'd meant. "Not Astraiya."

My teacher, Ms. Keller, glanced down at me, her innocent eyes blinking in surprise. "But your name is so lovely," she said.

"I don't answer to it anymore," I insisted.

I had a feeling my teacher knew of my past, because her eyes watered before she nodded and slowly agreed Raiya was just as suitable and lovely.

Either that, or she was unable to stand up to a child.

Still, I got what I wanted and with very little fuss, so I thanked her. As she smiled, for the quickest second I saw a small bubble of light appear between us, shimmering beside her heart. It was a strange ball of fire, one with several colors and wispy strands. I blinked and it was gone.

This wasn't the first time this had happened; I had seen those lights many times, and it always called me back to that moment when I nearly drowned alongside my parents in that terrible car accident.

It hadn't taken me long to figure out that seeing those heart-lights was a special skill I alone had; it was one of the reasons that when Grandpa told me the truth about being a fallen Star, I had no qualms about believing him.

I never knew anyone else who was able to see the little bubbles sparkle between the spaces and seconds between us.

Because I saw Ms. Keller's heart-light was cheery and somehow eager to please, I looked away in shame at my brusque assertion, before finding my seat in the back of the room.

That seat made all the difference in the world.

A tall, skinny boy, one whose hair was curled into short dreadlocks, sat in front of me. I was surprised when he turned around and met my gaze.

It was hard not to stare. His eyes were a smooth and dark brown, like the baking chocolate Rachel was always experimenting with at our small house. But even more than the color, I liked the kindness I saw reflected in them.

"Hey," he said, greeting me warmly.

It was never hard to see that Reggie was a gentle soul, always ready to take the bad and make it good, always ready to take the good and make it better. Even from that first moment, I knew that was true.

"Hi," I murmured, still staring at him. I was unsure of what he was doing and how I was feeling. *Why is he talking to me?* I wondered.

He cocked his head toward the teacher. "Ms. Keller give you any trouble?"

I shook my head.

"That's cool, that's cool. I didn't think she would. I don't like my full name either," he said. "That's why I tell people to call me Reggie."

"Oh. What is your full name?" I asked, unable to help myself.

He wrinkled his nose, irked but not deterred. "Reginald. Reginald Banks."

"Oh." I didn't know what else to say to that.

"My pops named me after a baseball player," he explained. "I think he was hoping I'd play."

I didn't say anything. Ms. Keller began talking, but I just sat there and listened to Reggie talk. He seemed like the kind of kid who wanted to talk, even if it meant trouble, and I liked that about him, especially considering how I barely wanted to talk at all.

"But I'm not going to," he continued. "I'm not good at it. And I don't wanna be a ball player. I want to be an artist."

"An artist?"

"Yeah, you know, like a painter or a street artist. One day I'm going to move to New York City or LA or somewhere big, and I'm going to make a name for myself with my art. But not Reggie, and definitely not Reginald. I want a new name for myself."

"What name were you thinking of using?" I asked, still curious.

He shrugged his shoulders, making his hair shake, too. "I don't know yet."

"Well, I guess you have some time to search for a new one," I said.

"True, true." Reggie smiled at me, a lazy smile showing white teeth against dark lips. "What about you? What do you wanna do?"

That was the moment I decided, from the lilt of his voice and the kindness of his face, that I genuinely liked him.

Suddenly, that spark of light came up between us, the one only I could see, and I gaped at him for a long moment, watching the power of the light as it held steady and settled against his chest. He didn't notice it, and he didn't seem to mind that I was staring at him, my mouth hanging open like a deranged lunatic.

I was used to seeing the heart-lights flicker and wink at me, before folding back into nothing but air. But Reggie's light held constant, and for the first time, I was able to get a good, long look.

Soulfire. The word came rushing at me from the back of my own heart, and I trembled at the madness mixed in with my memories.

"Well, Raiya? What about you?" Reggie asked again, his tone patient even though he seemed a little confused as to why I wasn't answering.

I clutched at my notebook, recalling the doodles I'd drawn. "Well … " I began, trying force myself to breathe properly in between my words. "I actually like to draw, too," I admitted quietly.

I didn't know what else to say. It seemed like a good place to start. And it helped that it was true; the art therapy classes Rachel had suggested to Grandpa Odd only a few weeks before were already a source of salvation for me, a respite from the pressures of living without my parents.

Reggie nodded toward my notebook. "Let me see."

I had already survived getting to class, so taking a chance on a stranger seemed less intimidating, even though I felt as though more was suddenly on the line. I handed him the book and held my breath.

I watched as Reggie glanced through them, the light of his heart still glowing and shimmering in different colors and moods. He nodded a few times, letting his gaze linger over some of my sketches. I watched as he studied a picture I'd drawn only the day before, a simple line sketch of two shadows reaching out for each other as a bright star in the night exploded around them. It wasn't bad for a first grader. At least, that was what I thought.

"Wow," he said. "That's really good."

I felt my heart swell uncontrollably. "Thanks," I whispered.

He gave me his lazy grin as he handed the papers back to me. "Awesome. I'll be able to work with you when we get to art class. None of my other friends really like it like I do."

His enthusiasm was catching. I finally gave him a tiny smile, one that seemed to crack my face from my recent, unrepentant neglect. "That would be great," I said.

THE STARLIGHT CHRONICLES

So that was the day Reggie and I became friends. He was my best friend, and I was his.

But after I broke Reggie's heart, everything was ruined.

Everything.

☼2☼
The Consequences of Losing Control—Part 1

"Hello, Raiya. It's always great seeing you," Dr. Dinger said, walking into the room. He folded my files under his arm as he reached out and shook my hand.

I shook his in return, amused by how much I liked him. I'd known Dr. Mark Dinger for a few years, starting when I first came to Apollo City.

Back then, I would lie awake in my bed for hours, listening to my heart squeeze the blood inside of it, wishing for death even though I felt a strange desire to stay where I was— hoping beyond hope that there was something greater yet to live for. Eventually, I would fall into dreams, where all light and darkness seemed to slide into a void.

It was as if I was searching for a reason to keep on living— a reason other than knowing my life had a price on it that I had yet to pay.

When I finally confessed to Grandpa what was happening, he was relieved. He told me he heard me thrashing about in my sleep.

That was when Grandpa told me the truth.

He told me the truth about how I was born from a fallen Star, a being of power who protected Earth. I had a growing power inside of me, one that would help fight off evil and save people from harm when I was older. He said all Stars had a duty, and since my power—the Star of Justice—had fallen, I would have to pay for my fall with my life.

23

I knew, partially from the way he'd said it, he actually meant that I would have to pay for it with my death.

Honestly, it was never a hard burden to bear, even learning the truth as a child. After surviving the car crash that killed my parents, I was ready to believe I should be dead anyway.

When I started seeing Dr. Dinger, the city's top cardiologist, I felt better.

Even when he told me the biological specifics behind my broken heart.

It was broken in more ways than one, apparently. I'd been born with a heart murmur, one that hummed a persistent song throughout my blood, one that I could no longer remember clearly.

Even though I desperately wanted to.

My mood stabilized in Dr. Dinger's presence; it was as if he was a marker, a sign, telling me I was exactly where I was supposed to be. Despite breaking Reggie's heart, my own came alive as Dr. Dinger predictably took my blood pressure, listened to my heartbeat, and ordered more tests.

I watched him as he worked. He was probably in his forties, but he seemed younger than that to me. I would watch when his eyes turned into slits as he smiled and laughed with Grandpa over sports or news or stories, and widened with ease and expectancy as he looked to me for my own input into the conversation. His voice was both warm and hard, like a teacher speaking through a script even as he faced the temptation to leave it. I had a lot of respect for him.

24

"Well, Raiya, can you tell me what you think brought on the pain today?" Dr. Dinger asked.

I met Grandpa's gaze for a quick second before I shrugged. "Could be anything, really," I lied.

"You didn't have a bad day at school, then?" he pressed. "I know school can be stressful, especially at the beginning of the year. My son has been complaining about it since he went back last week."

"School is okay for me. And my day wasn't all bad," I murmured.

That wasn't a lie. The day had started out pretty great, actually. Ms. Carmichael, my art class instructor, announced during class that Reggie and I were going to paint the new mural near the art room. All of the students in her class had submitted plans for the empty wall at the start of the school year, but in the end, the principal picked my design. Since Reggie had made suggestions for the color scheme, Ms. Carmichael allowed both of us to work on it during her class.

Personally, I considered it a huge honor. Years of art therapy classes allowed my work to become much more refined and clear. Working on the mural affirmed my improvement. And with Reggie working on the mural beside me, I also knew it would be fun.

At the news, Reggie and I exchanged a happy smile and quickly began transferring my design onto the empty wall outside the art room. We were excited; we cheerfully worked together with the familiarity of an old married couple, laughing and chatting and playing around.

25

Soon, all that changed.

When class was over, Reggie was unconscious, and I was curled into a fetal position on the floor, terrified and near tears.

The school called the ambulance for Reggie. They called Grandpa Odd for me.

Grandpa called the doctor.

And now, the doctor was looking down at me with his own patient kindness—no pun intended, even if it was appropriate—and I was unable to do anything to help myself.

"Well … " I shrugged. "I don't know, Dr. Dinger. Maybe it's a growth spurt?"

From the opposite side of the room, I could sense Grandpa's wry amusement.

"I suppose it's possible," Dr. Dinger said, glancing down at my chart. "You did grow quite a bit from last year. We can't rule it out. As you grow, your body will put more stress on your heart."

I only nodded; I didn't want to tell Dr. Dinger the truth, either.

If there was anything I wanted to do, it was go back to my house, curl up in bed, and force myself to think of nothing for hours on end.

Dr. Dinger unwittingly gave me what I so desperately wanted—after another round of drawing blood and tests, of course.

I glanced at the sheet and gave him a playful smile. "Only three tubes of blood today?" I asked. "Why not make it four or five? I can donate some while I'm at it, if you'd like."

Dr. Dinger gave me a kind pat on the shoulder. "Just three for today. It's for the best," he said. "If you are going through a growth spurt again, we'll have to watch everything more closely. That murmur could turn into something dangerous if we don't."

"I know," I said. "You've told me before."

"I've also told you before that if things didn't improve, we should consider putting you on the transplant list." He glanced over at Grandpa Odd. "I'm afraid I will have to recommend it, at this point."

Despite everything that happened earlier, my heart sank even further. "If you think it's best … "

Dr. Dinger nodded. "I do. I'll get the paperwork started and have it sent over to your grandfather while you get your blood drawn."

"Thank you," Grandpa said. "As always, we are grateful for your work, Doctor."

Dr. Dinger smiled. "And as always, it's a pleasure to see you, Mr. Cole." He looked back at me. "You, too, Raiya."

He tipped his head to me once more, almost giving me a sweet little bow, and headed for the door.

"Hey, Dr. Dinger," I called out, unable to help myself. "Have you heard anything about Reggie?"

Dr. Dinger faltered. "Reggie?"

I knew I'd caught him off guard, but I also knew he was aware of what I was asking. "Sorry, I mean Reginald Banks. He's my friend," I explained. "He came in earlier, before me … you know, in the ambulance?"

"Oh." Dr. Dinger shook his head. "I don't know much, to be honest. I'm not his doctor. But if he's here, I'm sure he's fine. Apollo City has a high reputation for healthcare. You might even be able to see him, if his family is here."

I had a feeling that dealing with Reggie's parents would be hard. I'd met them before, and they were nice people. But I knew they would ask me questions, and there was no way I would be able to give them answers. Not any that would make sense, anyway.

After all, how do you tell someone that you broke their son's heart, and then tried to fix it, only to make it worse in the end?

There was a small *beep*, and Dr. Dinger quickly said his goodbyes, already replying to the alert. I frowned; I didn't think I'd ever seen him with a beeper like that before. I had a strong temptation to ask him about it.

But after another second, I decided not to ask him any questions; after all, I didn't want to answer any questions from him.

Leaving the hospital could not happen soon enough, I silently decided.

I remained still as three techs worked to get information and blood samples from me. I never winced when the needle entered my skin anymore; the small pinch I had felt when I was younger was gone. Grandpa used to help hold me down, but I no longer needed to worry about troubling him. My Starlight Warrior power had something to do with that; I could heal myself, letting the light inside of me flow over any flaw, capturing and holding it, before rendering it perfect once more.

As the last tech left the room, Grandpa cleared his throat. "You might want to be more careful with that," he said.

"I think I know that already, from what I did to Reggie," I muttered.

"So, you *did* try something?"

I blanched. "I don't want to talk about it," I whispered. "I'm sorry. It's too soon. Maybe later."

"Later" was one of my favorite words. It would delay any pain I had, often long enough for me to get out of handling it at all.

Grandpa seemed to sense my shameful resolve. He stared at me, hard in his own way, but I knew the second that he decided to give in to me. He indulged me in all sorts of ways, from his dramatic readings to help with homework to new painting supplies—but only rarely did he release me from my Starlight defender training.

"Either way, the techs might notice that there's no blood rushing out when they take the needle from you," Grandpa said carefully.

I tried not to show my relief. "Alright."

"Some pain is good, Raiya."

"The pain of a broken heart isn't," I insisted, suddenly frustrated all over again. "That's why it's called 'broken,' not something else."

"I said good, not perfect."

I nodded, knowing that he was right, and it was pointless to argue with him. Grandpa was right a lot of the time, and even if I gained some ground against him, it hardly ever seemed to be enough for a full victory.

In all honesty, I didn't know if I ever really wanted to win against him. He told me one day that, should I overcome him, I would be sadder for it than anything else. When he said it, he gave me a soulful, sappy expression; he looked more like a haggard old man without anyone left in the world than his usual self, and for that reason, I didn't have any trouble believing that he was right about that.

"Why does Dr. Dinger call you by my last name?" I asked him instead, deciding that changing the subject was the best option.

Grandpa blinked innocently at me. "What?"

"Dr. Dinger calls you 'Mr. Cole,'" I reminded him. "Why? That's not your last name."

"Oh, it's fine," he said. "It's nicer than being a Johansen. I have better memories attached to 'Cole.'"

I remembered that Rachel had known some history of her father, before he left. She was the one who told me the truth about my grandmother, and how she was now gone. But it was still really confusing sometimes; when I asked Aunt Letty about it once, she sneered at me and simply said, "Families are complicated, Raiya," before lighting up a cigarette.

"Rachel says that your last name is actually Skarmastad," I said.

"Oh, that's nothing. It's in my mother's family."

"She says you're related to the founder of Apollo City," I said. "What's his name? Ogden, right?"

"Yes, that's it. I guess you could say I'm related to him," Grandpa said. He waved his hand, dismissing the issues. "And the other fickle heirs, too, the ones that all squabble over the city matters. Which reminds me, I have to go to a legal hearing about that today. The Time Tower needs another paint job, and all of them are, not shockingly, out of the country."

THE STARLIGHT CHRONICLES

I laughed. "I'm surprised they get up in arms about everything like that, if they're not even here for it."

"Money is an important tool in this world," Grandpa said with a shrug. "As much as you and I were not born into this world the same as others, we still have to work with the tools we are given. The Skarmastad family has no money. It's all in their charity works."

I frowned. "That seems weird."

"With Ogden no longer in charge, the money from his businesses goes to charity, so long as the heirs battle it out in court," he said. "In fact, it's by their charitable contributions that you and I can come and see Dr. Dinger."

"That's surprising," I murmured. "And confusing."

"When you're older," Grandpa assured me, with that kind look in his eye, "I'm sure you'll come to understand why I distanced myself from them."

I grinned. "I can't imagine you fighting over money." My grandpa always seemed to be one of the most generous people I knew. Even if it was not with money, he never seemed to hold back anything from me.

"I'm not a fighter. Perhaps I am more of a negotiator. And it's to their benefit that I am. If the government pays for their new coat of paint, they'll be happy. And so I must go," he said. "You, on the other hand, should to get back to the house and check in on Rachel. She's almost finished with her last semester, and she's getting frustrated with the business end of things."

"She's another one I can't imagine would argue over money," I said, thinking of my cousin and her generous nature. I glanced down at the bracelet Rachel had given to me shortly after I came to live with them. She was seven years older than me, and when I first met her when she was fourteen, she quickly pronounced herself my champion. I never forgot her gift to me. The bracelet was lovely, too, with its small silver and purple beads.

Behind me, Grandpa nodded, chuckling. "She's more likely willing to give everything of hers away, all to make someone feel better. It's good she suffers through her business classes, even if they are theoretically counterintuitive to her nature."

"I can't imagine that any business of hers would thrive for very long if she didn't charge for anything," I agreed.

"That won't stop her from finding a way to do it," Grandpa said. "Now, let us go then, you and I—"

"—when the sun is stretched across the sky," I finished, playfully hopping off the blood donor bench. I bypassed the cookies and headed out of the hospital.

As Grandpa turned to head into the heart of town, he cleared his throat.

I glanced over at him expectantly. "What is it?"

"I won't press for details about what happened today," he said.

"Thank you," I said, vastly relieved.

"But you must promise me, Raiya," he said, "that you will *not* use your power again. At least, not until we are certain you have full control."

"I wasn't planning on it," I replied, slightly irritated. I'd already shown him I had my control back. What more did he want?

"Your power has grown," he said. "And that is to be expected. But you have a lot of power, as a Guardian Star. The more you lose control, the more chance it has to cause problems."

"What do you mean?" I asked. "I've learned to control it, most of the time. I mean, I know there's trouble sometimes, but so far nothing has been too bad … " My voice trailed off as I thought of Reggie, stuck in his coma.

"It's not enough," Grandpa said. "You know the cost of power. It attracts those who would seek it for their own gain. You know I can protect you with my own power, and I do that as much as I can."

I squirmed, thinking of how hard Grandpa had worked in the last few years, suppressing my power's increasing fluctuations. "I know."

"Do you want me to put another seal on your power?" he asked.

Quickly, I shook my head. I never admitted it to Grandpa, but part of the reason I was as eager as I was to control myself was because I hated how it felt when he would use his power to suppress mine.

Grandpa was not a Star like me, I knew. He was an ambassador from the Celestial Kingdom, sent to find other fallen Stars and help them with their destinies.

Every time he placed a seal on my power, I would watch, transfixed by his own darkened blend of inner light, as he gently laid his hand on my wrist and sent a blast of his power rushing into me. It left a scratchy feeling around my wrist, and as much as I understood his concern for me, I still hated his assistance.

"There are limits, Raiya," Grandpa said, drawing me out of my thoughts. "As your power grows, you will no longer be able to be under my full protection. If you find yourself in a situation where you cannot control it, the demon monsters will come to feed on your Soulfire in droves, especially the *bakreel* and the *fenfleal* demons."

I shuddered. I did not want to think about that. I'd never fought one before, and I was not looking forward to doing so.

"Once they come, they will seek you out if you give them enough of a beacon. And we must hold that off as long as possible. You're not ready yet," Grandpa said.

I clenched my fists; it wasn't like I *wanted* all this to happen. "I'll be careful."

He only nodded, much as I had done back in the hospital.

☼

35

After saying my farewell to Grandpa, I headed down the streets toward the northern district of Apollo City where we lived. Our neighborhood was older, some parts crumbling and colored in graffiti, but it was home to me. I glanced down the halls of different colored brick buildings, amazed at how they could make me feel at home, even as they always failed to do just that.

Our home was an older house, with three floors and a small flat roof; it was more like an apartment building, but its grand, Victorian-style windows made it seem more like a mansion of sorts. It was fairly large, easily catering to our small, mixed bag of a family.

When I walked into the house, I heard Rachel grumbling in the back room. I strained my ears to listen, deciding that if she wasn't frustrated over her math homework, I would go and check in with her; if she was, I would go upstairs and let myself fall apart.

"If I can check in with Mom here, I could have them tear down the front porch and the overhang, and then … "

Rachel's murmurings were clearly not about math—so far as I could tell, anyway—and caught my curiosity enough that I headed back to see her.

"Hi, Rachel," I greeted. I think I was too optimistic, because she frowned.

"Raiya," she said. "What are you doing here? School's not over. I mean, they don't have half-days this early in the year, do they?"

"No," I said, giving her a small smile as I put my bag on the table beside her. "I left early. I had … an appointment."

Rachel's golden-green eyes went soft. "I'm sorry to hear that," she said quietly. "Are you okay?"

"According to the doctor, I am for now," I said, trying to cheer her some. "What about you? You look a little frustrated."

"Well … " Rachel gestured back toward her notebook. "Honestly … I met someone today."

"Someone?" I did not like how that sounded. "Who?"

"His name is Lee Reynolds," Rachel said. "He's a friend of Josh's, that guy I used to date from my study group, remember?"

"Uh-huh." I wrinkled my nose.

"Come on, Josh was nice enough," Rachel insisted.

Josh had been a "nice enough" guy, if you thought it was nice for him to forget to show up on dates, to call Rachel at all hours of the night asking for help with his homework, demanding she come and see his baseball games, even if she had work or class.

I merely arched my brow and sat down. "Well, if this Lee guy is friends with Josh, I hope he's a friend in passing."

"Josh had his flaws," Rachel murmured with a delicate and modest blush. "But he's still very popular."

I scoffed. I knew enough popular people from Rosemont to know that was an empty accolade. I grimaced, thinking of Courtney Knox, who was in Ms. Carmichael's class with me. Courtney was the quintessential popular girl, the kind who made her life easier by making other people's lives harder, and Reggie and I were constantly on her list of those other people.

I had a feeling she was probably telling everyone in the school I'd attacked Reggie and sent him to the hospital on purpose. She probably even had a story ready where I did it because I "didn't want to work on the mural with just anyone," which is what she thought I'd said when I turned down her offer to help with the mural.

Courtney was the main reason I disliked a lot of popular people, but Josh acted just like her on so many accounts, I had a hard time not hating popular people in general. They all seemed too self-important, too insufferably narcissistic. When Josh broke up with Rachel, it was well worth the week of her crying just to be rid of him.

"Well, Lee seems like a good guy," Rachel said, drawing me out of my tangent of thoughts. I was glad for it, too. I didn't want to think of the depressing situation of junior high social politics I was going to find myself in when I went back to school any more than I wanted to think of Rachel's ex-boyfriend.

"Let me guess," I said. "He likes your cooking?"

"Well … " Rachel's eyes glittered, dazzled and amused in her own enchanted way. "Technically, my baking."

There was no stopping my cousin's romantic enthusiasm. "So he ate the cookies you took to your study group?" I pressed, suddenly wishing I could have some of Rachel's cookies myself.

Appropriate, considering I'd just given blood and everything.

"He ate nearly all of them," Rachel confirmed, and I slumped forward. "He says I should start my own bakery."

"That's what you wanted to do anyway," I reminded her. "You were talking with your boss to add some things to the menu where you work now, right?"

Rachel instantly lost her enthusiasm. "She didn't want to hear it." She sighed and turned back to her paperwork.

As I studied her, Rachel's Soulfire sparked at my study. I saw her gold and jade mix of light, watching as it colored over with frustration and longing.

I wondered what she thought of Lee.

Rachel was getting closer to her twenty-first birthday. I knew it had been a while since she'd dated Josh. Maybe she was serious about dating again.

If that is the case, this Lee person better be good enough for her, I thought.

Such a thing did not seem possible. But at least Lee liked her baking. Josh had derided Rachel for wanting to bake all the time. He called her a housewife in the making, and one that would end up broke, too.

After I overheard him say that, I dreaded his visits and phone calls; I knew Rachel's homemaking skills better than anyone else, including her financial savvy, and I was glad when he was finally gone.

I was *really* glad when Josh was gone, actually. No one who undermines the requirements to running a home knows how much it means to have someone like Rachel, especially for people like me.

I watched as her Soulfire flickered again, this time with determination.

"What are you working on?" I asked.

"Lee was pretty adamant that I could open a business," Rachel said. "He's done it himself, working as a self-employed mechanic down at the docks, helping with repairs and some engineering needs."

"There will always be a need for repairs," I agreed, thinking of some of the vessels I could see when I would walk around Lake Erie's beachfront. This part of Ohio was known for the shipping industry.

"Lee says that people will always need good food, too," Rachel said.

I nodded approvingly. "And you make great food, Rachel, whether you're cooking or baking."

"Thanks." She smiled brightly. "So … I was thinking about maybe starting up my own coffeehouse. Maybe even here, you know, in the house. Lee even said he could probably help with any construction I would need."

"I can see that," I agreed, even though I had to cringe at the thought of all the modifications our house would likely need. "You like sweets, but people want more diversity in their menus. That's a good way to get it. And you could easily try new things all the time, and switch it up seasonally. I think you would even enjoy the challenge of paperwork, like the kind you have there."

"I'm working through the rough draft of a business plan now," Rachel said.

"You're doing math on your own? Willingly?"

She sighed. "I had a bad day at the restaurant with Kathy. Even my friend Holly isn't happy with her rotten attitude this week, and Holly has never had trouble getting along with other people."

"And that's especially saying something, since Holly's been very happy lately," I replied, recalling Rachel's various conversations about her friends at work. "She's the one who is getting married soon."

"To the love of her life," Rachel said, her expression melting into another happy, wistful, daydreaming look.

I loved Rachel and all her bubbliness. But just then, seeing her joy at others' bliss, and watching her Soulfire sparkle with longing at the thought of a new boy, only made me feel terrible.

Reggie's haunted expression flashed across my mind, and as much as I had tried to ignore the memory of what happened, I was brought face to face with it once more.

It was time for me to leave.

"I'm going to go," I told Rachel. "So you can work. I mean, it's not like you'd want my help with it anyway. I need Chelsea and Ayah's help to get through Algebra II."

"Where are you going?" Rachel asked. Worry came back into her gaze. "If you were just at the doctor's, you shouldn't go far."

"I can take care of myself," I assured her, as kindly as possible. "Besides, I think I'll just go take a walk for a little bit."

"Why don't you stay home and paint some?" Rachel asked. "You haven't added much to your collection lately."

I thought of the myriad of paintings I had up in my room. It was a real testament to my inner turmoil that I didn't want to paint. It was my most consistent remedy to bad days.

"I could," I said, "but I'd like to be outside for a while. After all, it's not every day I get to wander around during school hours."

THE STARLIGHT CHRONICLES

Rachel nodded slowly. "Alright," she agreed. "But be careful."

"Thanks." I wished her good luck with her project before heading out.

☼3☼
Truth Demands a High Cost

Shoreside Park was a large park, just a block or two down from my house. There were plenty of rocks and trees to offer me shelter from the outside world, allowing me to delve further into my own.

As I sauntered past the playgrounds and wound my way through the trees, the park itself was proving to be a prudent decision. I relaxed at the sight of the clear skies, watching as the horizon blended with the far-off mist of Lake Erie. In the distance, I could see a small, rounded rooftop in the distance, blinking back against the hot afternoon sun. It was the Lakeview Observatory's planetarium. I thought about heading over, before I remembered that it was closed for repairs.

That was a shame, I thought. Grandpa had taken me to see it a few times, back when I first moved here with him. I thoroughly enjoyed it, but our visits tapered off as my interest grew. I always thought that was a bit odd; if I was a fallen Star, why wouldn't I want to learn about astronomy? Grandpa assured me that the science of this world was not prepared to answer questions that I would ask.

Recalling my own inner bemusement and befuddlement at the initial realization of my power, it wasn't hard to believe him.

It was very easy to believe in that moment, considering Reggie was stuck in a coma at the hospital, there was likely nothing science could do to explain how he got there.

I groaned. Suddenly, that was all I could think about—how my power led me to this place, how I'd broken Reggie's heart, how his Soulfire imploded, how when I tried to stop it, he collapsed and everything inside of me crumbled along with him.

I made my way further into the woods. There was a small, grassy area behind a patch of trees, where Grandpa would teach me to learn to control my power.

I had to wonder, as I stood among the familiar trees, if I had come to this place, my old training grounds, drawn by a subconscious need of sorts.

Looking down at my hands, I curled them into fists. My power quickly appeared, wrapping my hands in violet light. None of the crackled sparks left my hands; it rested there, ready and waiting.

An inward rush of healing power ran through me, lending my body supernatural strength. In that moment, there was no doubting my power, no doubting my struggle.

"I've grown a lot," I murmured, pleased at the strength and confidence my palms exuded, "since the first time Grandpa brought me here."

The first time I trained, I was close to eight years old. I was terrified, and honestly, Grandpa didn't help much. He started

45

off by telling me that I would need years of discipline and focus and study, all to master my skills and rule over my power.

"Why?" I'd asked, looking over at him. "If this is my energy, and my own power, I can just control it, can't I?"

"We are no more capable of controlling our power as we are capable of choosing who we love," Grandpa said. "If you are going to do that, you will need to practice. You will need to learn to control yourself, and use your power—your mind, your emotions, your determination—to channel it into proper action."

I remember looking skeptical. "That doesn't make sense."

"Sometimes, for things to make sense, we have to have faith first," Grandpa replied. "You have not yet learned that there are things logic and reason are unable to account for. You are young in this life, Astraiya."

"Raiya, please," I corrected him. There was something about the way people said my name that I didn't like. It reminded me of my failure, of my status as a fallen Star.

"Raiya." He nodded at me approvingly, as if he seemed to like it better, too. "Now, let's begin with the basics, shall we?"

I nodded. "I'm ready."

"Are you?" he seemed to be joking with me, but I knew already that the answer had a lot of weight behind it. "If you're ready, you must be willing to accept things."

"I told you that I believed you," I said.

46

"One of the first things that you must accept is that not all of your questions will have answers—and the next thing is that you must believe the answers you search for you will find, often in their own time and often in their own way."

I didn't hesitate. "I can accept that."

He studied me for a long moment, as if checking to be sure that he believed it, too, and then he nodded. "As you say," he finally replied, and began to teach me to focus my power.

Meditation comes first, he'd said. People who win are people who know what they want. Meditation would lead to motivation.

That was easy enough for me, back then. I knew all I wanted was to stop being afraid.

But as I worked, seeing my own inner light spark and glimmer, a ghostly sort of shine in the emptiness of human life, I knew I feared it, and yet, I knew it was right to fear it.

I could not leave fear behind, so I vowed I would always have control over myself—my powers and heart and emotions, all of them. I would prove Grandpa wrong; I would make him proud of me.

Fear would not control me.

THE STARLIGHT CHRONICLES

Years passed, and I never wavered in my endeavor.

Not until now, I thought bitterly, opening my eyes once more.

I stood in the middle of the woods in Shoreside Park, realizing I had heard Grandpa's instructions as an eight-year-old, but I understood them better as a thirteen-year-old.

It wasn't enough to know what I wanted. After the incident with Reggie, I knew I had to want the *right* things—even if I was afraid. Especially if I was afraid.

It's time to rededicate myself, I thought.

If I was truly going to gain complete control over my powers, there was only option left.

To protect myself, and others, I would have to be alone. Forever.

It was a devastating surprise to realize that.

But it made sense. I would have to face my enemy—and my life—alone. I'd been born into this realm to protect it, and that meant protecting it from me, too, if duty demanded it.

Besides, what difference would it really make, to push my friends away? There were already barriers too big to climb and too wide to cross between us. I couldn't tell them the truth about who I was, and I never even tried. They would just be hurt in the end.

All I could do now was control the degree to which the damage happened.

So I would be alone.

I have always been alone, I thought. Even before my parents died, I had not known them very well. I knew my mother's smiles and her warm embraces, but I did not know her past, I did not know why or when she had fallen in love with my dad, nor did I know what had drawn my dad to her, and I did not know what they did for work. I knew them by their routines, by their expressions; I did not know them from their values or their stories.

I have always been alone.

Even with Grandpa, I was alone. He remained one of the few people I knew, but even his Soulfire never wanted to appear to me. Rachel and Letty were fine additions to our family, with their care and concern evident—each in their own way, of course, as Letty was still on the hunt for her own one true love, as her last couple of marriages ended in divorce.

I have always been alone.

The reality of Reggie's loss especially shook me, and shook me hard. It was worse than losing my parents—for all I had loved them, I had only known them for such a short time, and I had taken it for granted. Reggie and I had been friends for nearly six years, and in that time, I had loved him as a brother, as a best friend. My greatest sin was in loving him at all, not that I could have loved him as anything more.

"I am alone," I whispered, still listening to the hum of the power in my hands. "I have always been alone."

And then that still, small voice sang out to me.

I am waiting for you.

The words from that night came crying back to me, cutting through my meditation. I gasped, letting my power go, allowing it to flood over me as I fell to my knees.

I was pulled back into that moment when I lost everything of who I thought I was.

I was watching out of the car window as we passed through the Norwegian countryside. We were winding our way through several miles (or kilometers) of dark, twisting roads. I remember looking out the window, staring at the small girl who looked back at me. Twinkles of stars glittered at me from my reflection, shimmering all the more brightly as the sun slipped from the sky.

My dad looked back at me. "You can get lost in your pretty eyes," he warned me playfully. "Be careful."

"Dad," I said, giggling. "Come on."

"I'm not kidding," he assured me, before he gave me a smile and then turned his attention back to the road, and I studied the window again, wondering if my dad was really telling me the truth.

I wondered even then who I was, and who I would become. My hair was short and pushed back behind my ears, the loose locks glowing a golden ginger in the moonlight. I saw the stars reflected in my eyes, my pert nose, breathing in wonder against the glass.

And then before I could realize what was happening, I heard my father yell, heard my mother scream; I felt the unbelievably fast whiplash of the car as we bounced over a guardrail.

"Stop!" I cried, unable to believe that I could really say anything at all. "Mom! Dad!"

The windshield suddenly burst open. Water began to chill my skin. I looked back at the car window, where my reflection had been perfect and lovely only seconds before. It cracked and shattered, and I felt my own scream die in my throat as water rushed into my open mouth.

I choked and gurgled as the car continued to sink. There was a small pocket of air in the car, as we twisted away from the surface. My mom managed to grab me, to pull me free from my seatbelt.

It was too hard to look over at my dad's face. I saw the stream of blood coming out from his nose, and he was too still as I studied him out of the corner of my eye.

A rush of breath left him, bubbling up to the top of the water. It was then that I felt the malevolent onset of death. My dad was gone.

My mom was going limp as she reached for the door beside me. She wanted me to escape. "Astraiya," she murmured softly, weakly, as she fell under the rising water level. "Go."

"No!" I was frightened. "Help!" I cried out again, the water muffling my scream once more, before finally consuming me as well.

I don't remember getting out of the car. I don't remember the door opening, or anything getting me out. All I could think of when I thought of that moment was the utter emptiness of my heart, as all the light curled up inside of me.

And then it died.

I felt it all slowly drift away, all of it pass me by, even as it all passed through me. I seemed to be able to see myself, looking through the water as much as I had been studying my reflection in the car window earlier.

Then I faded away, and I was nearly all away when I heard it—that voiceless whisper against my irregularly beating heart, the power of it pulsating a new song into me.

"Let there be light."

I heard it. I heard it, and then I saw it. I was suddenly back in my body, and I was looking up through the night waters to see the light of the moon.

But it wasn't the moon that was shining. It was a man. It was a man full of light and truth, and he was waiting for me.

He reached down through the waters as they parted. I saw his eyes, crystals full of fire and ice, all power and all goodness.

I saw the spark of his Soulfire resting between us, as he reached down for me.

He took hold of my wrist and then spoke. "I am waiting for you," he said, his voice lovely and terrifying, gentle but thundering. It was just like the voice I'd heard in my heart, but somehow even more.

"Adonaias." I coughed and sputtered, and images began to flash across my mind. A whole life passed before me in an instant, and I recognized it as my own. I watched myself as a Star burst through my mind.

I was wearing celestial robes of white, armor of silver; with a sword at my side, with wings on its hilt. My hair was long and golden and bright, held back by shining starlight; I was a Star, a protector of Earth, a precious gem in all creation.

There were fantastical creatures by my side—dragons and griffins and birds of all elements and colors and styles; Stars and angels, seraphim and cherubim, with other heavenly creatures all calling out and exuding songs of joy and power and peace and goodness.

Astraiya, Lady Justice.

I watched Adonaias as he faded away, and different people took his place. I saw rescue workers and ordinary people and doctors all swim through my vision. All of a sudden, I had to battle for what was real, and what was true, and what would consume me.

The memories of that night had stayed inside of me, as much as I had tried to chase them away.

Still, I could not escape the truth. I was alone, but I was not alone.

Not in that moment, and not in this one.

I am not alone.

I opened my eyes, allowing the last tears to dry up.

Shoreside Park came back into my vision. I could see the clarity of the light as it lit up the details of each blade of grass, each leaf hanging from the different trees, each little rock and pile of dirt and fluffy cloud. Colors seemed sharper, more bright, and more alive.

I was alive. I was hurt, I was in pain, but I was determined.

I did not need a mirror or a reflecting pool to see my face. I knew who I was—I was the Star of Justice, a fallen Star, a Starlight Warrior who would protect Earth from the

THE STARLIGHT CHRONICLES

devastation I'd caused by my previous failures. I had been given a second chance to do my duty, *and I could not fail.*

"Adonaias," I whispered. "I am coming."

That was the truth. I no longer wanted to stop being afraid. It was a good and right thing, to be afraid of the Prince of Stars, and being cast away from him. I loved him, and there was nothing more that I wanted than to be with him again.

And if I ever wanted to see the Prince of Stars again, I had to give my all, and I would give all and more to see the one who was waiting for me, to see the one for whom I was desperately searching.

☼4☼
Paying Attention to the Wrong Things

The next few days passed quietly. I stayed home, unwilling to go back to school. I did not want to miss class, especially so close to the beginning of the school year, but more truthfully, I did not want to go back and see my friends right away.

I wanted to mourn them first. So I did. I stayed home and stayed sad.

Have you ever thought about how inconveniencing it is, to mourn for something? Even if you haven't already lost it?

The persistent thought of everything I was losing, everything I was drawing away from, all of it—everything hit me hard. Every time I thought about Reggie, or Chelsea or Jeff or Ayah, or anyone else who had ever been kind or friendly to me, I felt sick.

When the mourning became too much, I lost myself in my work.

Grandpa left me alone, as did Rachel. So did Aunt Letty.

I was glad for all of this, as I embraced the time by myself, relearning that to be alone meant to be free.

I trained, working on my fighting and my focus. I meditated, sitting in my room and pushing all thoughts out of my mind.

I worked on my paintings more, allowing myself to stay up late into the night to relieve the despair that seemed to settle into my soul.

I tested my power in small doses, molding it into different shapes, working it into different weapons. Grandpa didn't think I was ready to fight the demons, but if fighting them brought me one step closer to my goal of seeing Adonaias again, I was determined to see that it was done.

All I wanted to do was my duty.

That was all I wanted.

That was all I told myself I wanted.

But, as soon as I walked back into Rosemont, my friend Ayah Rashid came running up to me, and my determination inexplicably waned.

"Raiya," she called happily, and I felt my stomach reel in renewed sickness.

Ayah reached out and hugged me. When she pulled back, I had to fight off a smile. With her long hair falling behind her like a shining, black waterfall, and her large, innocent eyes, Ayah looked every part my perfect foil.

"Hi, Ayah," I said, determined to be polite and professional, and as least personable as possible.

"You're back. I was so worried for you," Ayah said. The rich hazel of her eyes glittered simultaneously with both worry and cheer.

Ayah wanted to be a fashion designer, and I think a large part of that was because she could have easily modeled her own clothing line. She was taller than me by a good five inches, with a much more willowy stature. Even with her sense of style curtailed by the standard Rosemont Academy uniform, she carried a sense of the exotic and adventurous with her as she bounced down the halls.

What I liked most about her was that she saw the beauty in everyone else and never hesitated to let people know it.

In her own way, of course.

I clearly remembered the time she told me everyone would be amazed at how beautiful I was, if I would only brush my hair back out of my eyes properly.

I grew out my bangs even longer after that, just to infuriate her. Playfully, of course. But I grew used to the protection they offered me, and I decided to keep them.

"Where have you been?" Ayah asked me.

I gripped my hands around the small briefcase I used as a book bag. "Sick," I replied, not wanting to be rude even though I knew it would make it easier for her to hate me.

"Are you feeling better now?" Ayah asked. She looped her arm through mine as we headed toward homeroom, something she had done countless times.

I eased away from her. "No," I replied. "So you might want to stay back some."

"You know I'm not worried about that," Ayah said with a grin.

"You might want to consider worrying," I said. "Look what I did to Reggie."

At Ayah's sudden frown, another layer of guilt washed over me. Ayah was easily one of the most beautiful girls in our school, and anything I did to make her seem less obstinately lovely only made me feel worse.

"You *did* do something to Reggie, then?" Ayah asked carefully. "I didn't want to believe Courtney when she started talking about it, but … "

"Um … well, uh, it's complicated," I said, blushing. "He, uh, caught me off guard, you know, with everything, and then, I think I caught him off guard and … everything just happened badly."

This was the first time I talked about it with anyone, and I realized immediately that I was going to have to come up with a better script.

I didn't want to lie, but I didn't want to tell the truth. After all, I *couldn't* tell the truth.

Ayah persisted. "He caught you off guard? What do you mean?"

"Well, he was trying to tell me stuff, and … " I felt my neck burn in embarrassment.

"He asked you out on a date, didn't he?"

There was something even *more* depressing about how she asked that.

But I nodded, avoiding her gaze. It was, sadly, the truth.

I was about to explain to her that I didn't want Reggie to love me that way when Ayah's Soulfire blossomed up in front of her, and it seemed to dim with the news.

Is she upset for me? Or ...

Suddenly, I felt dumb. Very, very dumb.

I never paid much attention to my small group of friends; I mean, I had never assumed that we would be anything but friends. There was no need to assume that we wouldn't be, either. After all, that was how we worked together. That was how it had been since the beginning.

Soon after meeting Reggie, I met Chelsea Hartman. She sat through my afternoon classes in our elementary years, helping me with computer stuff, science, and a lot of the math involved in both. When she sufficiently tutored me, we often worked together on our assignments.

In addition to her love of science and computers, Chelsea had a genuinely wonderful talent for music. She convinced me to sign up for the school's orchestra, since she didn't want to go to the practices by herself.

I think she was underestimating herself, personally.

But, since Rachel thought I'd enjoy the music part anyway, I went. And once Chelsea and I were at orchestra practice, two hours before school began, we met Jeff. After bonding

60

over musical codes and patterns and playing our instruments (the violin and harp for me, the viola for Chelsea, and the percussion for Jeff), he quickly became our favorite part of class.

That was third grade, when Jeff moved down from Maine. I remember Reggie being happy to get another guy into our smaller group of friends. I was his best friend, but he didn't want to hang out with just girls. With Jeff, it allowed us to work in groups of four, so we never had to worry about being awkward with someone we weren't used to—not unless the gym teacher made us switch, of course.

Because teachers always had to make us feel uncomfortable, at least some of the time.

It wasn't too long after Jeff came to be a part of our group that Ayah arrived. She came to Rosemont when her father got a new job, working as a consultant for some big company in Apollo City. She arrived just in time to join our group when we needed to put on a presentation together, and she offered to help us make costumes. Her skill, along with her ambition, secured us the top grade for our history class.

After that, the rest was history.

Or, at least, so I'd thought.

As I stood there in the hall, watching Ayah's Soulfire flicker, I realized she had feelings for Reggie—the ones I knew I would never have.

"I can't believe he actually asked you out," Ayah said, before I could say anything. "He'd mentioned it a few times, but I thought it was just a phase or a joke or something. No offense," she quickly added.

I waved off her concern. "I wish it was a joke," I assured her. "I told him no."

"What?" Ayah, for all her own feelings in the matter—the ones I noticed she wasn't admitting to me—was genuinely confused. "Why did you say no?"

"Because we're friends. We've always been friends. I don't want to date him."

Her Soulfire flickered again, with renewed hope.

Maybe that was all I needed to do before, I thought. *Tell Reggie something that would've given him hope.*

Obviously hitting him with an uncontrollable blast of my power had been the wrong way of doing it.

But as tempting as it might have been, I quickly discarded the idea. I didn't know for sure if talking would have worked. And what hope could I honestly and rightly give Reggie? I knew he was not the one who was meant for me.

I was determined that Adonaias was the only one I would ever be meant for, and I never wanted there to be anyone else.

Ayah took my arm again. "Tell me everything that happened," Ayah said slowly. "Why did he go to the hospital?"

I hated that I would have to lie to her, but I hated that she wanted me to talk about it. That made lying easier.

I shrugged. "I don't know."

"Did you just reject him and then he started to choke or something?"

Something.

Ayah continued, seeming to think aloud as she rambled on. "I mean, he hasn't been back to school since the ambulance came. Courtney said you attacked him. I didn't believe her at all, of course, but when you said … "

I snorted, bristling at the mention of Courtney. I'd been right about her, obviously.

As Ayah rambled on, I pulled away from her again. "I have to get caught up on all the work I've missed," I said, feeling cowardly as well as shameful. "We can talk about this later, okay?"

There it was: "Later," again. My favorite word.

"Fine," Ayah huffed. "But only because we have other things to discuss. You're still coming to my science class today, right?"

"What are you talking about?" I asked, genuinely confused. "I have science last period, not fourth."

"Come on, Raiya. You promised that you would help me with the presentation for my project in Mr. Adams' class. It's our first big grade, and it's due today. Remember?" Ayah pouted prettily, but I remained unmoved. I didn't really remember the project she was talking about.

"What project?" I asked.

"Mr. Adams' class. The biology presentation assignment?" Ayah prompted me to remember, but I shook my head. She pursed her lips. "I knew I should have tried to call you sooner. It's the fashion show I designed, with all of the lobster shirts. I made three shirts with the digestive, cardiac, and neuro systems on it. Chelsea is coming to help, and you said you would too."

"Oh." That honestly sounded like something I agreed to in a dream more than anything else.

"So it's fourth period," she said. "You'll be able to come, right?"

"Yes, I guess so." I nodded. "That's my math class. Mrs. Akers doesn't like me any more than I like math."

"Great!" Ayah returned to her cheerful, bubbly self, and I felt a rush of guilt as I remembered I was supposed to break away from my friends. "Come as quickly as you can, so I can fix your hair."

And then it was time to leave.

"I'll see you later," I said, slipping away. I watched as Ayah's Soulfire twinkled back into the folds of air, hiding itself from me once more.

Even though I hated the thought of dressing up for her project, I was glad Ayah was distracted from her concern for Reggie.

I headed off to first period, dragging my feet, reminding myself all over again that I had to be alone. It was good for me to be alone.

I frowned; that didn't sound right. I fixed it.

It was *better* for me to be alone.

There, I thought. *That's better. Now, it's time to get to work.*

Naively, I considered it my own good fortune that I had art class for first period. There was something I just loved about art. I knew that Rachel's suggestion for art therapy had been a lifesaver, but I doubted that was the sole reason I loved it.

There was just something about making the world a more beautiful place, something about seeing something for what it could be, rather than just what it was. I loved the idea of possibilities, and I was in love with my own imagination in many regards.

Whenever I would draw, I would continue until I was happy with the results. I saw this in my own collection, the one I'd been working on for a long time.

Maybe it was Reggie's compliment on my work, way back in first grade, or maybe it was more, but I had several stories running in my head that only seemed to come to life when I painted.

THE STARLIGHT CHRONICLES

In my sketch notebook, my pictures ranged from a large sailboat of sorts, traveling across the universe, led by a dashing captain, to a nebula full of baby starlight. There were some with people that reminded me of Stars. I had one of my own Star, playing the harp with another lyrist beside me, all while a shadow watched over us with envy. I once painted the death of a Star—that one always made me deeply sad—and I saw the Pleiades constellation as a living group of seven Stars, joyfully tending to the brightness around them.

I loved those stories. They sustained me in a strange way, so much so that I didn't even need them to be real in order for them to be true.

Once I got to class, I resumed work on the mural. Ms. Carmichael wanted it finished up soon, before our school's open house. I could understand her concern.

For the mural contest, I had submitted something quick, something easy, something very lovely, but still something that was largely filler material for me. I had never expected to win the right to paint the wall, as much as I was pleased by it.

As I walked by the art room, I was further pleased to see that it was still untouched from when Reggie and I worked on it. With Courtney making up stories about what happened, I was worried that Ms. Carmichael would allow her to "help" me.

The period began, and I worked thoughtfully and thoughtlessly, allowing the paint to puddle in my fingers and splash up onto my face. I never really wore makeup, but, as a kind of joke, I enjoyed getting paint on me; it was truly a way to add more color, more texture, rather than hide away my face.

Just as the paint itself made me smile, I felt at home in a space of time in which I was more or less free to dream. I was able to slip away to another world, one that was truly my home.

The hour of class slipped by, largely without my noticing, before Courtney's voice broke through my concentration like a spell.

"What are you doing? That's not what you were going to paint."

I whipped around, already feeling shame-faced and caught.

"Huh? What?"

Courtney sneered at me. She was indeed very beautiful; on some level, I would say she was too pretty, because she seemed to think she was entitled to a lot more than she actually was. I watched as her bright blonde hair bounced in layered curls, and her red-lipped smirk transformed into a vicious smile.

"I said, that's not what your design is supposed to look like," she said, crossing her arms as she leaned against the classroom doorway. "I knew you'd cheated to get your design picked. You were planning to change it all along, weren't you?"

Stupefied, I glanced back at the picture I'd been working on and fell silent.

I'd painted a face of sorts where one of the larger stars should have been. I stared, momentarily full of wonder at the picture before me. The man had penetrating blue eyes and a crown of feathers on his head.

I didn't recognize him at all.

Didn't I? I frowned.

There was something familiar … but …

"I'm going to tell Ms. Carmichael," Courtney said, snapping my attention back to the current moment. "And then she'll disqualify you and pick a new mural picture, like she should have when you attacked Reggie."

At his name, I felt the ache in my heart rise up again, agonizing and awful, and even more so because it was unexpected. I felt unspeakably terrible that I had caused such pain.

That I had caused such pain …

Gasping, I suddenly clutched at my chest. I heard Courtney berate me, telling me to cool it with the theatrics, before everything slipped away.

This time, I didn't push the memories away.

THE STARLIGHT CHRONICLES

It was that day again—the day Reggie and I were working on the mural.

At the beginning of class, when he showed up with the art cart, full of all the bright and subtle shades of color we required, I let out a celebratory cheer.

"Wow! How did you get this?" I asked him, grinning. "Ms. Carmichael is notoriously stingy with her supplies."

"Only for classes, when she can't play favorites," Reggie said. He gave me a wink. "But fortunately for me, I happen to know that we're her best students, despite what Courtney wants to think."

I stifled a groan at the mention of Courtney. Reggie and I both knew she was one of the beautiful people of Rosemont Academy. Her mother and father both worked in finance, and since they were rich, she always paraded herself around as an expert in everything, and unfortunately for us, she considered herself an artist. She had thrown a well-choreographed tantrum when Ms. Carmichael selected us to paint the mural.

Seeing my best attempt at a non-reaction, Reggie laughed, letting his now-long dreadlocks bounce. In all our years of school, he never liked getting his hair cut, and he never felt the need to change himself. I purposefully would change my hairstyle from time to time, as a joke between us, always teasing him playfully when I did. I'd done it as recently as that morning, too, with the half-bun I'd worn to school.

"Come on, Ms. Carmichael thinks she's a handful, too," Reggie said. "I heard that Ms. Carmichael's hoping to get sent back to the elementary grades after this year, just so she can avoid dealing with Courtney ever again."

"I can't blame her for that," I muttered. "I know Courtney is unlikely to forgive me after this."

"Courtney's never liked you," Reggie said, "because you have dignity. You've never tried to buy other people's affections with gifts or flattery or money or your body, like she has. You're happy to get along with everyone, but when people don't want to get along with you, you stand up for yourself."

I silently agreed. "Well, I don't have the time or desire to put up with people who don't really like me. Or don't even want to try to get to know me."

Reggie nodded. "True, true," he said, before handing me a handful of pencils. "Come on. Let's get your outline graphed, and we can work our way in from each side."

Several long moments passed while we started sketching. I was just finishing the thicker outline of the famous *Starry Night* moon when I spoke up again. "You know, either way, I hope Ms. Carmichael will stick around. She's a nice teacher." I reached for a new pencil; the one I'd used to draw on the cement block walls had ground down the point it was next to nothing.

As I studied the progress we were making, grateful to be under the hall's slanted skylights, I saw Reggie shrug on the other side of the mural. "When she wants to be."

"You're really going to complain about her, after she's allowed you to take her cart full of supplies out here?" I arched a brow at him as he glanced at me, and he laughed.

"She could be better," he remarked.

"True, true. But there's no use forsaking the good in search of the perfect," I said.

"You can't deny perfection is an admirable goal."

I wrinkled my nose. Reggie sounded too much like Grandpa Odd at that point; Grandpa was always saying things like that, pushing me to do better with my Starlight Warrior training. "I can't deny that," I replied to Reggie, "but pretending there's nothing good where there *is* something good is something you can't deny, either."

"Dang, girl. You got me there. Or at least, I think so," Reggie conceded. He grinned good-naturedly, and I was unable to resist smiling back.

We worked as we always did, first in quiet and then both humming along to whatever music we happened to be overhearing on the art classroom's old radio. We ended up laughing and singing along with the song, whatever it was, and I barely remembered because I was enchanted with the project at hand.

"You know," Reggie said between songs, "I'm surprised you put this design up for the mural. I would've thought it would be one of your own painting sketches."

71

"I don't know how I would feel putting one of my own paintings up in the school where everyone can see it," I said.

"Why? Your stuff is so good," Reggie said. "You should totally show it off in public."

"Rachel says when she gets her own restaurant, she's going to hang up my work."

"Good!" Reggie smiled. "That's perfect. Your work is quality stuff, Raiya. Even if it's a little … dreamy."

I shot him a hard look. I knew Reggie liked my work, but he always seemed to find something wrong with it.

Reggie preferred his own work, which was modern and simple, full of lines and shapes. He called his own work "neo-expressionist," and I laughed at the joking seriousness behind it. I always thought that particular style looked more like a stained-glass window than anything else.

I hoped Reggie would like my work better after I finished my intended collection.

"My own artwork has its own series I'm working on. And anyway, this is a classic," I told Reggie. "*Starry Night*, by Vincent van Gogh. It's a safe choice, even though I'm convinced Ms. Carmichael selected it because of your suggestion to change up the color scheme."

"You don't like the idea of it as much as she did, do you?"

It was as if he could read my mind. "Well," I said slowly, "it's not like it's my own work. I'm up for trying a few new things."

Reggie paused for a moment, and, for no real reason at all, I suddenly felt the need to panic.

"Well, if you're up for trying a few new things," he said, "how about you and I go out on a date together?"

The pencil in my hand slipped through my fingers. My body, already chilly from the school's overzealous air conditioner, went cold. Time seemed to slow down, torturing me as each second suddenly felt like a spear, each one dragging slowly through my skin. Pain increased through me as I slowly turned around to face him, dreading what I would find.

It was there, of course. The bright little bubble of light, dancing gleefully in front of his heart. It swelled, as Reggie kept his eye on me.

The colors were breathtaking. He stepped closer to me, as I stayed still, unable—or maybe unwilling—to move.

I saw him take my hand as if I were watching the scene instead of participating in it. I saw him look down into my eyes, much like he had that first day we met.

"Well, Raiya?" he asked. "What about it? What about us?"

"Huh?"

In many ways, it was good, I guess, that I was shocked and scared beyond responding rationally.

Reggie and I knew each other well enough that there was no mistaking his question. I knew I couldn't play it off as a joke, as much as I might have wanted it to be one. I also knew that I would not run away, as much as I wanted to, because it would dishonor everything about me. But I couldn't tell him the truth, either—and there was no mistaking the truth.

At the core of my reaction, I instinctively knew the truth: He was not the one for me. And telling him would destroy all the good inside of him.

I had the future of his heart in my hands, and yet, Reggie was still staring at me, waiting. Just waiting. How did he not know I was deciding his fate?

My hands began to shake as I looked back at him. Just like that first day, his Soulfire flickered before him. It was even more bright than before, full of hope and patience, eagerness and curiosity.

He began to lean over, his eyes half-closed, and I knew he wanted to kiss me.

Meanwhile, I was having trouble telling myself to breathe again.

Finally, with just a breath between us, I clenched my hands into fists.

"Reggie—" I started to reply, but as soon as I said his name, his heart began to change.

It was like watching a star implode on itself. The bright light dimmed, first slowly, and then faster and faster. The little wisps and flutters and flitters, all the colors dancing around the core of his light, went dark and still.

"No!" I moaned, unable to stop myself from mourning.

Reggie stiffened. "You don't have to say it like that," he grumbled. "There's no need to be rude about it."

Before I could assure him I was not trying to be mean—even as I could not avoid it, it seemed—Reggie's heart plummeted into despair and disappointment, and my own heart began to explode in pain.

Before I knew what I was doing, I gripped at his chest. I felt my power rush out of me before I knew what I was doing. "Don't," I said. "Don't be hurt."

Reggie struggled to get away from me. "What are you doing?"

What am *I doing?* I remembered wondering that before my power lit up.

"What in the world? What's wrong with you?" Reggie's voice was suddenly afraid.

"Stop," I cried back, as though I was yelling at time more than Reggie, and myself more than anything. I needed to stop what I was doing—even though I didn't want him to be in pain.

"Stop it!" He began to fight me again, pushing at me, still unable to shake me. I screamed and threw out another burst of power, watching as his Soulfire stilled.

Like fire caught between the seconds, I had the entire essence of his being trapped in stillness.

"Raiya!" he cried. "Raiya!"

"Reggie!" I yelled back, unable to stop my power from overwhelming him.

Suddenly, I felt my fingers crack, my right hand surge with excruciating pain.

I was terrified that I had caused such pain.

That I had caused such pain ... again.

Memory faded into longing, and I saw the blue eyes, the ones on the face I'd been painting, and screamed.

"Raiya, stop!"

Hearing Courtney's sudden cry, I blinked, and blinked again. The scene cleared before me. I was standing in front of my painting, in front of the exploding star, the one that now carried the face of a man with a feather-crown on his head.

Or at least, that's what *had* been there.

"What in the world? What is wrong with you?" Courtney screamed.

Ms. Carmichael was suddenly at the door, her eyes wide and terrified, I found my fist curled into the wall, with the wet paint encasing my broken knuckles.

76

As Ms. Carmichael began asking me worried-angry-sounding questions, Courtney kept on yelling about how I was insane.

All I could do was breathe deeply, desperate to assure myself I was still in control of my power. I was so caught up in the rush of adrenaline that I didn't even realize it wasn't my power I needed to watch—it was my heart.

Before Ms. Carmichael or Courtney could say anything else, I ran off. I didn't really know where I was going. All I knew was that I had to go.

☼5☼
The First Time I Transformed

I ran until I couldn't run anymore.

I was upset, I was crying, and I was pretty sure I was going the wrong way. As I finally slowed down to catch my breath, I laughed at the thought.

Where could I go, really? There was no way to run from who I was. All I knew was that I had to go, and I wanted to go somewhere where I would be free.

I didn't want to go home. Grandpa would be there, and I already imagine the disappointment on his face. I could feel the seal of his power crack dangerously as I continued to run.

I didn't want to go to the hospital.

I had a feeling, even as much as Dr. Dinger strangely steadied me, he would not appreciate me dropping in unannounced. *Especially*, I thought, *with that new beeper of his*. It seemed like other things weighed on him, and I didn't want to add to his stress. He was a good man.

I stopped running at last. I blinked the wetness out of my eyes, flustered to realize I was back in Shoreside Park.

"Why am I here?" I asked aloud, my voice scratchy and sore. I wondered if I was yelling at myself. The last time I'd been at the park, I had meditated in order to find some peace. As my latest spasm showed, that clearly wasn't enough to control myself.

I thought back to what Grandpa had taught me. Meditation was the first step to finding a way to win, the first step to figuring out how to get what I wanted. I had to identify it, and then I had to focus on it.

"Meditation is used to find meaning," Grandpa said.

But meditation was only the first step. Meditation was used to find meaning, meaning should inspire motivation, and then motivation led to movement.

"Well, I'm definitely moving," I muttered.

As I continued walking, setting off toward the marina, I worked through the full exercise.

What did I want most?

Originally, I'd wanted to stop being afraid. There were other things I wanted, too—contradictory things that would never be reconciled.

I wanted my friends to be safe, I wanted a normal life, I wanted to be free.

But if I had to say what I wanted *most* of all?

Most of all, I wanted to see Adonaias again. I wanted my task, no matter what it entailed, to be over with, so I could get back to him and the Celestial Kingdom, where the other Stars were.

But that was a wish, and I needed a plan. I needed to know how to get back to him.

I needed the truth.

Why did I have to pay for the mistakes of my previous life? Was I really going to have to push all of my friends away? How would I get back to Adonaias after I fulfilled my mission? And what, exactly, was my mission, besides fighting off the evil demons and other monsters that sought to steal souls and twist all light into darkness?

Each question I thought of was somehow more terrifying than the last.

"Either way," I murmured to myself. "I want the truth." That was the best blanket answer I could give myself.

So finding answers was to be my motivation.

Where did I begin my search?

I'd talked with Grandpa Odd about some of this before, I recalled. He told me that I had been the Star of Justice, and that I had fallen to Earth in order to recapture the Seven Deadly Sinisters, the ones who had escaped from the heart of my Star.

But they weren't here yet. I knew that from Grandpa, too. I also knew that others would come before, to test me, to haunt me, and to try to stop me.

What else?

He'd told me before that not all my answers would come right away.

It was all too much, I thought. My heart couldn't take it. And the pounding pain of my hand was distracting me.

I had to wonder what Courtney thought when I'd shoved my fist into the wall. I made a mental note to buy some medical tape and a wrist guard, so Ms. Carmichael and everyone else would think I'd gone to the doctor.

But I forgot all of that as I glanced down at it. I had been ready to use my power to heal myself when I saw my wrist was shining.

Shining. *Shining*. Letting out light from underneath my bracelet, like it was the most normal thing in all the world.

Well, I thought with a wry smile, *it probably is somewhat more normal for Stars than humans.*

I studied for a moment. The light, only slightly shadowed by the remnant of Grandpa's broken seal, cut into my skin in the shape of a four-point star, humming with not only power but purpose. It was as though my body, incapable of holding in my power, had finally allowed it to break free, and the power had marked its doorway with its brightness.

Cautiously, I ran my fingers over the mark. Something about it called out to me.

I pressed on it.

All at once, I felt the light as it leaked out from the mark, winding its way around my arm and all over my body. The light became a tangible thing, wrapping all around me and permeating through me until I was completely encompassed by it.

When the light cleared, I glanced down to see myself.

My mouth dropped open.

My arms were covered in wrapped gloves, colored a distinctive blue and white. I had a matching tunic on, with purple details lining down its length, to the point where it fluttered out like a skirt; protective armor weighed on my body, and matching boots suddenly shielded my feet. Wings sprouted out from my back, and I nearly fell over as I felt their weightless burden.

As I steadied myself, a pair of wings fluttered out from either side of my head, and two chains draped across my forehead in a grand manner, lending me a grace I didn't have and a majesty I didn't deserve.

"What is this?" I wondered, and as if to answer me, I felt my heart swell with supernatural awakening.

I looked back down at the mark, peeking out from the bottom of my glove.

I was no longer surprised. The mark on my wrist had changed, along with the rest of me. It was no longer just a silver, four-point star. Another star lay over the top of it, one that shone with a blue-violet color.

I recognized it, slowly but then certainly.

The Emblem of the Prince.

I held my hands out in front of me, looking down at them in shock.

As I stood there, a fiery red feather flickered into my field of vision. Reaching up, I tucked it between my fingers carefully, almost hesitantly. It was soft and smooth to the touch, and as I held it, I thought of the face I'd been painting earlier.

I haven't been paying attention, I thought. Those bright blue eyes flashed across my mind again, full of pure and holy fire.

This was his feather.

"Why do I have it?" I asked.

My heart gave me the answer before I could even begin to imagine it.

Because he gave it to me. Because he loved me.

Tears threatened me once more. "And I destroyed him," I realized.

Either that, or his love for me destroyed him.

Did it really matter how, in the end?

It all makes some strange sort of sense now, I thought, as the feather in my hand tingled with warmth. I'd been thinking about pain when I hurt Reggie.

It seemed only natural—*supernatural*—that the situation would trigger memories of my previous life experiences.

I glanced over myself once more, still shocked and sad and unsure.

Time seemingly slowed as I stood there. The world around me had changed along with me, too. There were shadows at the corners of my vision, while the world itself seemed much more contrasted, as if I were looking at the world through a camera filter. I saw strange colors, auras, limping around the surrounding landscape.

"What … is this?" I wondered aloud, watching the scenery around me.

Before I could receive any answer or even try to think of one, I heard a loud *crash!* from behind me.

I whirled around, looking for the place of the explosion. I must not have been used to my wings, because the shift in direction made me nearly fall over. I steadied myself, allowing my feet to sink firmly into my boots. I found myself facing the marina, when the small feathers at the sides of my head twitched.

Suddenly the air was full of people, calling for help.

I have to help them.

The instinct to move toward the danger pushed me, and I consented to its rule; I rushed forward out of the woods, heading toward the source of the sound. Looking around, I realized that a building project had collapsed near the marina, on the other end of Shoreside Park. A cloud of ominous smoke billowed up from the ground, forming a pair of evil eyes as I looked on it.

I blinked, but the eyes were still there.

Another name came rising up out of my memory, but still needed time to form completely.

That was when terror hit me, along with a sharp realization. While I wanted to help the workers who were now trapped, the ones who were now calling for help, I didn't even know I *could* help them. After all, from all my training, I was expecting that I would fight off demons and monsters and minions.

Not disasters of this sort.

The wind pressed around my wings. The long, white feathers caught it and pressed back, giving me a sense of determination I didn't know I had.

I jumped into the air and took flight, easily floating several meters off the ground. Excitement bubbled up inside of me, and I wished I would have been able to take a picture.

From my new vantage point, I could see more of the marina; it looked like a small crew of workers had been drilling down.

I frowned momentarily at the thought. *Why would anyone be drilling underneath the lake?*

I shook my head, clearing my thoughts. The reason why was not as important at that moment. It only mattered that the men and women who were down there would survive.

Taking flight once more, I soared over to the area, grimacing as the smell of putrid smoke grew closer. I dropped down onto the ground, close to a bulldozer.

Around the side, several of the construction workers were fleeing. Some were calling for help.

One of the people screaming was a man in a lab coat. He seemed oddly out of place, but then again, so did I.

I ran up behind him, listening as he called out for his friends, begging God to answer his prayers for help, and whimpering about how much he wanted to go home to his wife and son.

As he waited for 911 to dial through on his cell phone, I wondered if I should do something.

Should I go up to him and ask? I wondered.

Before I could do anything, a young man with black hair came running up beside him.

"Dr. Harbor!"

I watched as the man looked up. "Lee."

"What happened?" Lee asked.

"We had a faulty circuit blow," Dr. Harbor said. "There are three of my men down there, along with my site manager," he said. "I can't believe this is happening … "

His voice trailed off as he turned around, continuing his nervous pacing.

Lee stepped up. "Where are they? I'll see if I can find them."

"There are three levels that we've been clearing out for the new lab; my workers are trapped down at the bottom, closer to the lake." He hung his head. "We were laying down the concrete for the hall today."

Lee nodded quickly. "Keep trying for the police," he said, and then he hurried off.

As Dr. Harbor stared around blithely, I decided it would be best to follow Lee.

It wasn't hard to sneak by Dr. Harbor, even with my wings and my strange outfit. As Lee hurried toward a worker's ramp and started to head down it, I quickly followed. When I saw that the ramp led down into the heart of the smoke, I decided it was time.

I reached out and grabbed onto Lee's shirt.

When he turned around, obviously prepared to battle with someone—likely Dr. Harbor—I quickly stopped him.

"Stay here," I ordered.

"Who are you?" he asked, first confused, and then somewhat angry, and then somewhat flustered.

I pushed him aside, and tried not to grimace; I'd only meant to get him out of the way, but I ended up slamming him into a wall of dirt and rock.

I made a mental note to watch my strength from now on. "Just stay here," I repeated as he struggled to rebound.

I headed away from him, working my way into the heart of the smoke.

Lee said nothing else to me, but as I lost sight of him, I hoped he was at least shocked enough to stay out of the way.

Quickly, I forgot about him. The ashen warmth wrapped around me at once, but I called up my power to help me keep it at bay. I was surprised when it worked, but I didn't have time to do much more than take a note of it, and then hurry through the half-built, half-broken mess.

Hoping I was not fanning the flames even higher, I carefully jumped down through some of the more complicated levels, tapping the beams of steel and metal with my boots almost playfully as I passed over them.

My power shone brightly, pouring violet light into the darkness. "Hello?" I called. "Anyone here?"

Anyone alive?

I didn't want to ask that question aloud, but it sounded loudly inside of me.

"Help!"

Hope flared inside of me at the response. I heard a cough and another cry follow the first, and I sped off, trying to get through the smoke.

After a long moment of checking floor strength (before dumbly recalling that I had wings) I saw them.

There were, as the man up top informed me, three men and a woman nearby. They were all huddled up together, with one lying unconscious on the floor.

"I can see you," I called. I was just about to tell them to get closer to me, since my power was able to hold off the smoke and dust, when they all turned in unison.

I felt my mouth drop open in surprise. Reggie's father was among them.

"Wha—?" I tried to recover from my shock, fumbling over my words for several seconds, before I remembered that he was an architect.

There was another rumble behind us, and I struggled not to show my fear. I knew I could protect myself and heal me, but I did not know the extent of my power or its capabilities.

As I saw my power flicker, I realized I also did not know its limitations.

Great, I thought bitterly. *This is going* so *well.*

Two of the men scooted closer to me, including Reggie's dad. "We have to save Gabe," he said, nodding his head toward the man on the floor.

"Okay." I readily agreed, but I almost felt like I sounded like a naïve fool. When I saw, even in the small light of my power's beam, that Reggie's father looked skeptical, I hesitated even further.

89

THE STARLIGHT CHRONICLES

"Can you carry him?" I asked Reggie's dad.

The woman spoke up. "Gabe is trapped under a fallen gurney," she said. "He's stuck. We'll have to leave him here."

"We have to try to do something, Lynn," Reggie's father said.

Why can't I think of his name? I wondered

The other man turned to me. "Can you do something, Angel?" he asked.

"Angel?" I frowned.

Before I could respond, there was another *snap* behind me, and out of the corner of my eye, I saw one of the wooden wall frames snap in two. The flames on the other side flared up.

In the added light, I saw that the lady was right. Gabe was caught with his legs under a large beam of metal.

I also saw that the men and Lynn were both looking to me. "Alright," I said. "Come and help me, and we'll see if we can get him free."

There was a bright bubble of light in my palm as I hurried to assess the situation. I decided I could try to cut the beam, but I would have to be careful.

"Get ready to pull him free," I ordered the men, and I was surprised that they listened. Apparently, people who are afraid and worried about dying have no qualms about listening to a barely-teenage girl dressed up in what looks like a cosplay outfit.

I shuffled my doubts to the side. I shaped my power into a blade and tried to cut through the beam.

I was met with plenty of resistance, but there was enough of a dip in the metal that I kept going.

Please … please let this work, I prayed silently, as I sharpened my power against it once more.

"Who are you?" Lynn asked, her voice clearly astonished even as she was being covered with more ash by the moment.

"No questions, please," I shouted, as I pushed the blade of light down further into the melting metal. It was so close, but still so far away from breaking.

A moment later, I felt my energy begin to dull. I stopped to rest, keeping my power steady, but slowed.

"What's wrong?" Reggie's dad asked.

"I'm not used to this," I admitted. Immediately after I said it, I wished I hadn't. The small amount of hope I'd seen in their eyes dimmed next to nothingness. "I mean, I'm not used to doing this in a fire," I tried to elaborate.

Reggie's dad shook his head. "Let's grab Gabe," he said. "Joe, Lynn, let's grab him and pull him while the lady works."

Despite the fact I knew I'd blundered, I felt a rush of pride at being called a lady. For a teenager like myself, it was nice to

91

be noticed on an adult level by other adults, especially one I respected as much as Reggie's dad.

"You almost done?" Reggie's dad asked, and I nearly jumped.

"Almost," I promised, nodding firmly. I went back to full power, only giving off a silent groan as I felt weak.

It was draining, really. My heart felt fear, like I would not be able to save everyone; my body tingled, with both power and weakness.

"There!" I cheered. Gabe groaned as the beam finally cut in half. I nearly burned off half his leg in the process, with the violet light of my power cutting close to him.

Reggie's dad, the other guy, Joe, and Lynn all heaved and grabbed a limb, and pulled him free. I was suddenly glad that there were multiple people, because I didn't have the fortitude to carry Gabe myself.

I panted some, coughing as my shield of light began to break down.

There were more rumbles and crumbles around us. I barely heard them as I tried to remember the way I'd come.

Help me.

I saw a twinkle of light at the top of my vision. "There," I said, pointing to it. "Let's head that way."

"What are you talking about?" Joe asked. "I don't see anything."

"Um … it's this way," I said, heading toward the light.

"No, there's a stairway over here," Joe insisted, tugging Gabe's arm to the right. "It's close to the elevator shaft. I say we go that way."

"But we need to go this way," I insisted.

"We're the ones who built this place," Joe snapped. "We know where all the emergency exits are."

Another teasing crackle behind me increased my worry. "Please, just trust me," I tried again. I believed in my power. I knew the truth. I wouldn't have come this far, only to fail.

I knew I had to follow the light.

"Why should we?" Joe asked, before I could reassert my orders.

Lynn placed her hand on his arm, as if she was going to try to reason with him. "Joe—"

"No, don't do this," Joe said. "Don't make this about niceness. Manners don't matter when you're this close to death. And this *is* a matter of life and death, and she's already admitted she's new to the game."

My face burned again, and the flames around us had nothing to do with it.

"She got Gabe out," Reggie's dad pointed out.

"I'm going to go and survive," Joe said. He dropped Gabe's arm, letting Lynn pick up the slack. "I know my way around this underground lab. You obviously don't. And you're crazy if you don't follow."

I didn't know what to say.

All I could hear was the pounding of my own heart, the flickering of the flames, and the creaking of the building's burning infrastructure.

"Let him go," Reggie's dad said. "You okay, Lynn?"

I barely paid attention as Reggie's dad looked back at me and gave a slight nod.

"You got us out so far," Reggie's dad said. "Lead us the rest of the way, Angel."

I felt myself nod in return, and that was it.

I led them onward toward the light, as my power carefully lit our steps, a few feet in front of us at a time. We didn't look back as we heard the corner of the building collapse behind us. I tried not to think about Joe.

The light ended up leading us to a small makeshift rig, one which held extra tools and cleaning supplies and other things I didn't recognize. It was attached to an automatic pulley, and I felt a rush of relief. The rig wasn't big, but once we could get up, we would be on the ground level.

"Here," I said, letting them get on.

"The electricity is out," Lynn called. "We can't move."

"I'll get it," I promised, and then immediately regretted it as I looked at the control box. I literally knew nothing about electronics, let alone wiring.

For a moment, I tried to lift the rig myself, pushing it. It barely moved. When I grabbed one of the thick steel cables, I wasn't able to pull it much more than a foot before my half-gloved hands began to shriek with misery, even with my power restoring them.

I was just contemplating using my power to try to jump start the pulley when there was a new type of rumbling.

"The dam broke!" Reggie's dad yelled.

As I looked behind us, I saw it: a wall of water came breaking through the building's layout, rapidly filling up the room.

If I'd had time to properly analyze it, I might have been glad that the water was coming; it put out the fires, for one, and it really helped to clear out the smog.

But staring down a wave made me shake.

Too many memories of that night in Norway, came crashing down on me, along with the water. I felt myself slipping under again, and I didn't know if I would have the perseverance to climb out once more.

"Come on." Reggie's dad gripped me, hauling me up out of the water by my arm. "Pull the rope now. The water will help us get to the top."

Reggie's dad stepped off the rig and grabbed the rope, and together, as I felt the water lap its way around me, we managed to get Lynn and Gabe to safety.

I barely thought about anything as we made it back to level ground.

As Reggie's dad and Lynn hurried to get Gabe to the nearly-arrived ambulance, I slipped back into the woods and watched from a distance.

I watched as Lee and Dr. Harbor, the people who had been on the level ground before the fire and the flood, answered questions and asked their own. I watched as Reggie's dad looked around, probably looking for me.

I watched as Dr. Harbor got the news that Joe had drowned, his feet caught in a broken stair.

I watched as my hands flapped helplessly, before clenching into fists.

And then I watched as the ground left from underneath my feet, as anger and sadness flooded my vision. I took off, flying through the city much as I'd run off from school—blinded, desperate, and barely paying attention.

☼6☼
Seeing, Not Looking

For the second time in less than a day, I was running away from my trouble.

Or was I?

I had a feeling, similar to the one I'd had earlier, that I needed to leave. But this time, there was also a calling on my heart—my broken, destitute, desperate heart.

Adonaias. Adonaias. Where are you? Where are you?

His name ran through me like an invocation, weaving itself around my broken heart like a rosary.

I blinked, and suddenly I was on the roof of my house.

Some part of me wondered if Grandpa was home, if Rachel was around, if Letty was close. But apparently, that part of me wasn't in charge.

I hurried down the stairwell into the house, heading toward my room.

Opening the door, the familiar scent of cinnamon chai and acrylic paint wafted to greet me. It did nothing to comfort me, nothing to stop me.

"Where are you?" I yelled. "Where are you? I want some answers, Adonaias!"

There was no answer. I glanced around the room, expecting to see something—anything—that might tell me that I wasn't

97

crazy, to tell me that I wasn't insane or hallucinating or poisoned, or who only knew what else.

My room was silent. My paintings, the various ones I'd worked on, circled the room, some of them half-finished, some of them in full living color. All of them were silent as I looked at them.

That was why I slumped over and cried, letting my wings fall over me.

I don't know how long I lay there, on my wooden floor, my fists pounding against it in alternating blows. My knees eventually did start hurting, and I felt my power flicker along with my consciousness. I shook it off, determined to stay alert, waiting for my answer.

An answer I never thought would come—and an answer that didn't come.

But it didn't come because there wasn't someone to provide it, and it didn't come because there was no answer.

The answer didn't come, because it was already there.

And when I looked up again, I finally saw it.

I gasped. There was that light again—the same one I'd seen that night in Norway, the same one I'd seen in the midst of the construction site, shining in the middle of water and fire.

It was everywhere and nowhere, a ghost of its familiar brilliance, touching on all my work.

I blinked and rubbed my eyes, shuffling my weight onto my knees.

I looked around my room at the paintings, and I saw them for what they were at last—not merely stories, not merely pictures, but memories. Memories and moments from my previous life.

The large sailboat that mapped out the growing universe. It was the *Meallán*, guided by the hand of St. Brendan the Navigator, who loved to laugh and play as much as he loved to work.

The Field of Lights carried the birthplace of Stars and human souls. I could almost see one of its caretakers, the Star of Hope, Lady Elpece, as she waved to me.

I was back in my Star form, before I'd fallen, playing the harp with another Star—the Star of Courage, Orpheus, who was in charge of my younger sisters, the Seven Starry Virtues.

Kneeling on my bedroom floor, I saw my other paintings come to life: I saw Adonaias, as he had me judge the captured fallen Stars and sentence them.

And then I looked to the other paintings, the ones which were only half-finished. I felt a familiar pull to some of them, recognizing my sister's portraits and the Star of Time and her castle of gold and light.

"They were mine," I said, barely able to feel myself say anything. "All of these are mine."

There was one I saw that caught my eye, the one where Adonaias reached forward from his own heart, out toward a fallen Star, one who I was supposed to judge, but for some reason, the Prince had stopped me.

I frowned.

The Star in that picture was not complete; I'd only angrily outlined his eyes at the time, before I had to get ready for school. But as I stared at them, I found myself falling into the scene.

And then, my heart shattered all over again.

I cried out before passing out.

It really said something, that I was not really surprised to find myself in the hospital when I woke up.

A sigh of relief passed through my lips as I saw I had reverted to my normal self, although instead of wearing my school uniform, I was wearing one of those hospital dresses that barely counts for clothing.

"This is not a good habit you're establishing."

Glancing over, I saw Grandpa Odd was sitting beside my bed. His fingers were tightly wrapped around the book he had in his hand—one of Shakespeare's works, *Othello*—and I could tell he was frustrated.

I couldn't blame him. After all, I was back in the hospital, likely waiting for Dr. Dinger to show up. My hand, the one that had smashed into the wall at school, was wrapped in a small bandage. I almost laughed as I looked down at it, avoiding Grandpa's gaze. I'd healed it earlier.

So why is it bandaged … ?

"This is serious, Raiya." There was an uncharacteristic sternness to Grandpa's voice, and I blinked up at him in surprise.

It was the same as last time, I realized. Grandpa knew what happened at school, what happened outside of the art room.

That was why my knuckles had medical tape strapped on them, and that was why I was here.

The incident at school seemed like an eternity ago.

"Don't worry about it. Please, Grandpa. And besides, I'd hardly call this a habit. It takes twenty-one days to make a habit, remember?"

Grandpa did not appreciate my attempt at levity. "That's just a majority consensus from pop culture," he scoffed. His joking turned sharp, fast, and I was more than a little hurt. "Besides, I know you have always been exceptional. Especially when it comes to things like this."

"Things like this?"

101

"Punching a sizable hole in a cement block wall, for one," Grandpa Odd said, nodding toward my wrist. "They want to bill us for that, you know."

I groaned. "Please don't tell Rachel," I begged. "I don't want her to think she'll be the one who has to take care of that, especially now that she's trying to find a way to get her own restaurant."

"I didn't tell her that," Grandpa said.

A flood of appreciation swelled up inside of me. It was important to know that while Grandpa was upset with me, he was still protecting the ones I loved.

Grandpa glanced around the room. "She might get an inkling about the health care bill, though."

I slumped over. "Great." My head fell into my hands. "I'll work it off, or I'll do something. Anything to help with it."

"It'll be alright, Raiya."

"Are you sure?" I asked, my voice barely a whisper. I glanced at him through my fingers.

He nodded. "Yes. But thank you for proving me right once again," he said. "You're definitely exceptional when it comes to avoiding the real issues."

"Real issues?" I was about to argue how medical debt could cripple Rachel's potential for life when he nodded curtly and continued on with his lecture.

"Yes. We have to talk about the issue of your supernatural powers."

It didn't take anything for me to know I was not going to like the following lecture.

"It's 'later,' Raiya," Grandpa said. "It's time for you to tell me what happened with that boy. Every detail, do you hear?"

"Please, don't make me," I begged. "I swear, it will never happen again. I can control it now. See?" I let my power pool out in my palms again, just as I had the last time. The healing rush was intoxicating if not necessary, and I was proud to see the power burned even more brightly. "It's stronger, too."

"I see that," Grandpa said, scowling. "Just as I see that the seal I'd placed on you is completely broken. I won't be able to hold back your power anymore."

"Oh." I didn't want to tell him that I was okay with that.

"This can only bring trouble, Raiya. I expected better from you."

"What do you mean?" I asked. "I mean, tell me. I know you're mad, but tell me why. I can't try to make it better if I don't know why you're upset, specifically."

"There is no making this better," Grandpa told me. The anger in his voice softened, but only minimally.

"Why?" I asked.

"Can't you feel it?"

"Feel what?"

He grabbed my wrist and scowled. "So, there is it," he muttered, looking down at the four-point star under my bracelet.

"It's the Emblem of the Prince," I said. I looked to expect some sort of praise or happiness from him, but Grandpa just looked wary.

"I don't know if this is a good thing," Grandpa said.

"I'm thirteen years old now," I reminded him. "And a Guardian Star besides. You told me that yourself. Why wouldn't my power begin to show itself more assertively? I can't hold it off forever, even with your help."

"You weren't supposed to worry about this yet," he said, making me wonder if he meant that *he* wasn't supposed to worry about this yet.

I straightened my shoulders, finally fed up with his temper. I had my own pride and dignity, and I had proven myself earlier. "I transformed earlier today. I know what I'm up against."

Grandpa sighed—that sad, slow sigh that I always dreaded. "I wondered about that," he said. "But it wasn't something that happened today. You've been here for the last three days, recovering."

"Three days?" I blinked, momentarily losing my focus. I glanced around, looking across the room for a calendar or a clock or something. Anything to reorient myself to the passage of time in the Mortal Realm.

"That's not the only thing you've missed," Grandpa said. "You've missed plenty of school, and some of your friends have come around looking for you. That fashion girl was one of them. She said you missed her project."

The project for Mr. Adams' class.

My mind seemed reluctant to stretch back into my school routine, but I forced it through a moment later. And then I sighed.

"Yes, she was quite disappointed, too," Grandpa drawled.

I tried to tell myself that it was better that I disappointed her, so it would be easier to convince her I wasn't a good friend in the first place. But that was an argument I would never win, one I would always lose.

"I think she got your other friend, Jeff, to help her instead," he added, his voice slightly softer.

Part of me wanted to know if Grandpa was really sorry for me, or if he was just trying to sound like it. He'd been the one, after all, who had warned me about having friends, and of all people, I was the one who knew how important it was for him to be right.

I slumped back against my pillow, trying not to let myself cry. "Is Dr. Dinger coming to see me today?" I asked, deciding it was best to change the subject.

"I'm not sure," Grandpa said. "But I'm not concerned about that. You said you transformed."

I nodded. "Yes."

"Tell me about it. What did you see?" he asked. "What did you see when you transformed?"

Since he wasn't asking about Reggie anymore, I told him the whole story. I left out the part about Reggie's dad being one of the men though. I didn't want him to follow that tangent back to my previous mishap.

I tried to meet Grandpa's gaze with my own as I talked, recounting the story in its near-fullness, but I felt my eyes keep slipping to my hospital blanket.

When I finished, I let the room fall back into silence.

Moments seemed to turn into hours, as Grandpa sat there, still and thoughtful.

Finally, he spoke. "What did you see around you?" he asked, repeating his earlier question.

"You mean in the underground building?" I frowned. "Nothing too unusual. I mean, who really wants to build an underwater lab in the first place, but still—"

"No. I mean, what did you notice about the area around you when you were transformed? What did you see?"

I shrugged. "I didn't really see anything unusual. Or at least, unusual by our standards."

The attempt at lightening the mood was lost again. Grandpa sighed. "You didn't see anything?"

"I don't think so," I said. "But I'm not really sure what you mean, either."

"Transform."

"What?" My mouth dropped open. "Now?"

"Yes." Grandpa Odd's eyes narrowed into dangerous slits, as he focused on the door to my room. He stood up and placed himself in the corner behind the door, securing the room. "Now."

He turned his snakelike gaze on me, and fear ran chilly down my back.

Scooting my legs out from my cover, I looked back down at the silvery mark on my wrist. It was for the best, I decided, not to ask again. Grandpa trained me hard, but he rarely demanded anything of me. It felt wrong, but it wasn't like it was hard.

A spilt-second later, the light inside of me came pouring out, coursing over me, covering my body in renewed power.

The rush was like nothing else. I marveled down at my new self again, dazzled by the violet and blue outfit that protected me, awed by the tiny wings that tickled at the sides of my forehead, and humbled by the somber, friendly, flame-colored feather mixed into my hair.

"Do you see it now?" Grandpa asked.

I almost smirked, watching him place a hand out in front of his eyes. He seemed to have a hard time coming to terms with my new level of power.

Instead of asking him about it, I glanced around.

Quickly, I realized what Grandpa meant.

Before, standing just outside of the art room, I hadn't noticed anything that was happening in the present. By the time I realized what was going on, my fist was three inches into the cement wall, blocking out a face my mind was unable to recognize even though my heart wanted to set him free.

I'd realized it some at the marina, watching the colors and auras of my supernatural senses flood my vision. I'd even seen those strange eyes, those eyes of evil, as they poured out from the smoke at the heart of the world.

Grandpa was right. The world was different now, especially now that I was different.

There was so much light and goodness in my power, and as I stood there, transformed, the room felt darker, more dull, and somehow more deadly. Outside, the auras I'd seen before were dappled across the city, a saturated mix of dark and light and every shade of rainbow in between.

"Do you see it now?" Grandpa asked.

I nodded. "I've seen it before, too," I said. "I just … "

"You've seen it, but you weren't really looking," Grandpa finished.

I bit my lip. He was right.

As usual.

"I see it now," I said quietly. At my admission, my own power seemed to dull somewhat.

"Raiya, you need to focus on more than just your power," Grandpa said, his voice less blistering than I expected. "You do seem to have control of it, and your skills have grown. But there is more than just the power you must control."

I have to control myself. Recalling the vow I'd made before, I clenched my fists. Power sparked and drizzled into air. I watched as the light folded away, blending into nothingness. I felt as though there was a vacuum clashing with the light, a fight between the warmth and the absence of it.

I met Grandpa's gaze. "Is this … is this the Void?" I asked.

He nodded. "We live in overlapping realms, Raiya. If you can feel the otherness of the Void, if you can see it, that's never a good sign."

I knew that the Void was the place to which the demons were banished, but that was the first time I noticed it in using my own power—and that was the first time I realized its seductive pull.

"What does it mean?" I asked.

"Your power is centered on justice," Grandpa reminded me. "You have the power to send the demons to their final place. That means that your power is most potent when you are working between the realms. Before you fell, you had no

109

trouble resisting its allure. You will have to watch that you don't fall to its power now."

"And if I do?" I asked quietly.

"Everything is lost," he said. "Every time you use your power, you are taking a stance that is dead set against everything the Celestial Kingdom works for. Their stance can be attractive in the moment, when you want something desperately."

I thought about the shadowed feeling I'd experienced earlier, when I felt the lines between good and evil grow more stark.

More stark and more terrifying.

"I can feel them, Raiya," he said. "I can feel the demons coming closer. But it wasn't supposed to be like this. The Sinisters—the ones you are called to defeat—are not supposed to come for some years yet."

I looked back at Grandpa as I pressed the mark again, letting the sharpness of my supernatural world soften into normalcy. "What do you mean?"

But I didn't need him to answer. I saw it.

I'd seen it in my paintings. I saw the Seven Deadly Sinisters. I saw them, as they blossomed out of the corruption of the Seven Starry Virtues, poisoned against me. Lady Justice lost her sisters, but tried to keep them. I'd imprisoned them inside my own Star, in order to keep them close.

And then they had escaped.

And I was supposed to die along with them. But we were saved, somehow.

The red feather flickered into my field of vision. *The Phoenix Star. The Star who had been reborn.*

Before I could remember his name, Grandpa sighed.

I pushed the past out of my mind. I didn't want to deal with it, or the pain it would likely bring. "What do we do now?" I asked him.

"We wait. The smaller demons come slowly at first, and then more and more quickly. We will have to watch for them more carefully than ever."

I nodded.

"In the meantime," Grandpa said, "I have your homework here. You might want to work on it. You're not going to finish school if you can't keep up."

A wry smile crept onto my face. "That's true." I thought about being a fallen Star, and having the kind of power that I did. "I guess there's no school elective for hero work."

Grandpa leaned back in his chair. "None that we can admit to, anyway," he said, before he opened *Othello* again.

☼7☼
They Come Slowly and Stay if You Let Them

Grandpa was right about the demons. They did come slowly at first.

It is a great trick of demons to get people to think that they do not exist. It is another great trick of theirs to show up in places where no one would ever expect them, and to ease into your life so subtly that if you do want to get rid of them, their claws are already deeply imbedded into your soul.

I also found out from my own experience that reality will not offer any help to offset their efforts; in fact, it will probably help them.

This was clear from the things that managed to distract me, enormously, from their creeping presence. The marina incident was one of them. I was pretty depressed about it, even though I did save people, but I was even more depressed when I read the news.

The first morning I was out of the hospital, I saw the *Apollo City Mirror* had picked up the story. The headline read "Government Construction Deregulation Leads to Marina Company Death and Mental Illness," which immediately upset me in itself. I read the article, biting my lip the entire way through, as the reporter painted the event as an example of government corruption and the result of big businesses cutting safety methods in order to save money.

"Who wrote this trash?" I glanced at the name on the report. Patricia Rookwood. I made a mental note never to believe anything she wrote again. After she treated the death of Joe and the near-death escape of Gabe, Lynn, and Reggie's dad (whose name I relearned was Tomas) as some sort of preconceived plot to kill people, I had no respect for her.

I was also very upset with her for her portrayal of the survivors. Luckily, the people I'd helped were the only ones caught down below before the fire started. But since they were the ones who did survive, their stories were given more emphasis.

That was where I came in.

I found out several people, including Lynn, were content to think I was a figment of their imagination or some kind of hallucination. Even though Gabe said it sounded like I was a guardian angel of sorts, Patricia Rookwood was quick to dismiss my help as a stress-induced vision, a sign of mental illness.

On some level, I was glad, actually, that no one really seemed to think my *Astroneshama* self was real. I didn't want the attention, and I didn't want to cause any trouble. I also didn't want the media blaming me unnecessarily, like they were doing to the man in the lab coat I'd seen, Dr. Harbor. He was the lead consultant on the project, as an astrophysicist and engineer who worked for Otherworld, Inc., the company who was trying to build an underwater lab down by the marina. The social backlash of the situation called for his firing, and his company seemed like they would be all too happy to give it to him.

113

THE STARLIGHT CHRONICLES

So the news report made me angry, and anger can be quite distracting.

But there were other surprises, too. It turned out Lee, the Lee who had been trying to talk to Dr. Harbor during the situation, was Rachel's Lee.

And yes, by the time I was released from the hospital and headed back to school, he was indeed Rachel's Lee. That was the first thing she told me after telling me how much she missed me.

"Raiya!" Rachel cheered as I came into the house. She bounded out of her chair and came over and hugged me tightly.

After several days in the hospital, I welcomed it. I knew Grandpa loved me, but he was never much of a hugger. When Rachel embraced me, I allowed myself a moment of vulnerability.

She was my sister more than my cousin in many ways. Even though there were seven years between us, Rachel was my best friend and my most ardent supporter.

"I'm so glad you're home!" Rachel said, the little golden flecks in her eyes glowing happily. "It's been so lonely here."

"I can imagine Grandpa and Aunt Letty aren't the greatest of company, considering how much Grandpa likes to stay in his room and how much Letty likes to leave for dates," I said.

Rachel laughed. "You know it," she agreed. "But I've missed you most of all, because you're the only one I'd ever talk to about boys."

"A wise move," I said. I put my backpack on the floor by the door. "I've missed you too, of course, and your tea more."

"I'll get you some," Rachel replied, as she hurried into the kitchen. "I've got to talk to you about Lee."

I nodded. "You know I'll be here for you when you need to cry about something."

Rachel laughed. "I'm not actually crying this time," she said. "Oh, and please don't mind the smell. I tried to make some gingerbread earlier."

I wrinkled my nose as I realized the house smelled like burnt cookies. "You never seem to get that one," I said.

"It must be made for you," Rachel said. "It doesn't like me."

"Oh well. You've got pretty much everything else down better than I do," I reminded her. "Maybe it's fate's way of feeling sorry for me. No one seems to like it except at Christmas, anyway."

Rachel laughed again, and it was a joy to see her happy. As I sat down, cupping my coffee mug full of tea with my hands, I hid my surprise when she told me that Lee had been the one I'd seen talking to Dr. Harbor.

Well, I guess this means I'll have to give him some approval, I thought, thinking of how he wanted to go in and save the others at the construction site.

It was for the best that I approved of him, anyway. Rachel had given him the approval to take her out, and she was already anticipating a second date.

"We didn't do much, you know," she said, "we just met here for coffee—Mom wasn't too bad, even though she was still here—and then we walked around Shoreside for a couple of hours. With me in school, I don't make a lot of money for a nice date."

"He probably would have taken you out somewhere nice if you'd wanted to go," I said. "Most of your dates are like that. They like to impress you."

"True. But he's a hero," Rachel said. "I would have insisted that I pay. And it's best to insist anyway, for the first date, so you let them know you like them."

"Is that how the game is played now?" I laughed. "Well, it's a good thing I'm not ready to date or I'd be at a disadvantage."

Rachel frowned. "What about your friend Reggie?" she asked.

I went still, and Rachel sighed. "I'm sorry," she said. "I know you've been worried about him. I thought maybe … maybe you were concerned so much because … "

THE STARLIGHT CHRONICLES

I shook my head. "No," I said. "I don't want to date him. He was my best friend."

"Was?" Rachel looked over at me quizzically.

"I mean, is. He *is* my best friend. Beside you and Grandpa, of course," I added with a smile.

She did not allow me to throw her off course. "He does like you though," she said. "Maybe you should give him a chance."

"No."

"Why not?" Rachel's prodding was gentle, but I still felt the sting of it.

"He's not the one I'm meant to find," I said simply, suddenly feeling stupid.

"How do you know?"

I shrugged. "I just do."

"What if you're wrong?"

"I'm not."

"But what if you're wrong?"

"I'm not."

"Come on, Raiya. It's okay to like him."

"I do. But only as a friend."

"Are you afraid of falling in love?" Rachel asked.

Of course I'm afraid, I thought. I was afraid of loving people at all. I'd lost nearly everyone I'd ever loved. And part of me wondered if it wasn't my fault.

I thought about that moment when I hurt Reggie, and then sent him into a coma to try to stop him from being hurt. I reached up into my hair, mentally searching for the feeling I had when I first transformed.

"Raiya?"

It wasn't like I could tell Rachel the truth. She didn't know about my supernatural power. She didn't know about my past as a fallen Star. She didn't know I was living through this life only to see its end, so I could be with Adonaias in the Celestial Kingdom again.

"There are other things I'm focused on right now," I said truthfully. I didn't want to lie to Rachel.

She watched me carefully, and I tried not to squirm. For a moment, I didn't think she would give up.

But then she let out a defeated sigh. "I never win against you," she said. "But I suppose you are still quite young."

I smirked. "That's the truth."

"But you will promise me that you will fall in love one day, right?" Rachel asked. "Please?"

I thought about the feather again, for some reason. "I think I already have," I said slowly.

"You have? With who?"

THE STARLIGHT CHRONICLES

I nearly jumped at her question. Quickly, I hurried to cover my slip up. "I meant more, like, you know, uh … I mean … I'm pretty sure I've already promised you that," I said. "That's all."

Rachel gave me a weird look, but she let it go. "Well, I hope you'll keep it then," she said. "Life would be very lonely without love."

Life might be lonely, but that doesn't mean it will be bad, I thought, slighted by her assertion that just because I didn't agree with her, I was somehow wrong.

As Rachel went back to discussing Lee, I glanced out the front window. And then I rubbed my eyes and blinked.

I thought I'd seen a quick shadow slither by.

It was hard to know if it was real, or if Grandpa's words about the demon monsters were influencing me. Was a demon coming already, to feed on my power?

As I sat there with Rachel, having no clear answer, I shivered and gripped my mug more tightly.

When you are depressed, the last thing you want to do is something that makes you even more depressed. Searching out demons and trying to figure out how to defeat them was more optional than mandated, so I didn't do it.

119

I did, however, have to go to school. And if that wasn't depressing enough, I had to face the second largest reason I didn't do more about the demons.

My friendships started to unravel.

And it was the worst sort of good thing I could live through at the time.

As I headed back into school, I have no doubt that it was Rachel's kindness and warmth that sustained me. At first, it was hard for me to believe that I had missed so much, and it was only the third week into the school year. But it became easier to believe when I reached my locker and I saw Ayah and Chelsea waiting for me.

"Hi, guys," I said carefully, both dreading and anticipating their presence.

Ayah frowned as she looked me over. "You're feeling okay, then?" she asked.

I nodded. "I'm okay," I said, feeling like I was lying, even though I wasn't really lying.

It's hard not to feel like you're lying when people ask those questions, and you give them the answer they would prefer. And you would prefer, too, if you're honest.

The truth was, I *was* okay. My heart, even though it was broken, was functional, and my body, even though it felt tired and hollow, was unhurt. I had a ton of homework to catch up on; I had missed several projects, including Ayah's for Mr. Adams' class. But really, what is homework in light of all the things I had to worry about? It was nothing compared to the blossoming energy residing inside of me, nothing compared to the harsh lines of good and evil I experienced in my transformed state.

Chelsea looked from my face to Ayah's carefully, and I realized Ayah was still angry with me, even though she knew she couldn't blame me entirely for what happened. She thought it was a health issue, after all.

Chelsea was more sympathetic. "I took notes for you while you were gone," she said, handing me a notebook. "Mrs. Akers' class especially."

"Thanks," I said. I nearly melted at her kindness, but I was determined to keep them at arms' length. That shadow I did see or didn't see earlier meant that I could be dangerous, and I would not put my friends in danger. And I did not want to send them spiraling into despair along with me. "I appreciate it."

Chelsea gave me a kind smile, letting her brown eyes sparkle behind her glasses. "I'll need it back later," she said. "I've been taking notes for Reggie, too, since he's still out."

"Yes," Ayah said. "He's still out of school. But I suppose you probably already knew that?"

I'd tried to check on Reggie before I was discharged from the hospital, but I didn't get a chance to. I didn't want Grandpa following me or asking me questions, so as long as he was around, I didn't try to sneak in and see Reggie.

"I did," I replied. "I hope he gets better soon."

"It might help if you told us what you did to him," Ayah said.

Chelsea gasped, and I just winced.

"Come on, Ayah," Chelsea said. "She didn't do anything to him. It was just some sort of medical problem. That's why he's at the hospital. You can't blame Raiya."

Oh, yes she can.

"Oh, yes I can," Ayah said. She pointed her finger at me accusingly. "She told me that she did something to him."

"I'm sure it was just something she did in order to try and help," Chelsea said.

"That's not what she said it was."

"I don't want to talk about it," I said, my voice nearly cracking at the sudden lump in my throat. "But I would never do anything to intentionally hurt him. Or you guys."

They were silent for a moment as I stood there. I finally handed Chelsea's notebook back to her. "I'll get the notes from someone else," I said. "You can save this for Reggie, okay? No need to worry about me."

I pushed the book into Chelsea's hands, unwilling to wait to see if she would take it or not. And then I turned around and walked away.

Each footstep felt like a cut to my soul, as though I was cutting ties with them altogether. Some part of me knew I was. The other part of me didn't want to face that reality.

As I walked away, Ayah called out to me, "You're just disappointing us even more, you know."

I resisted the urge to turn around, to argue that I was disappointing them in order to save them.

Before I could give in to that temptation, Chelsea began to scold Ayah. "You can't blame Raiya for how Reggie feels about her, either."

That topic nearly had me running.

I was glad Ayah switched her ire onto Chelsea, already denying her feelings for Reggie had any influence in this matter, as I turned the corner.

☼8☼

At the End, You Think About the Beginning

For all I was half-worried that I wouldn't be able to get through another day without having another power surge, especially as I was working on my mural, nothing came of it.

Maybe it was better I was depressed about everything, that I thought obsessively about how all my friendships were slowly crumbling into dust.

As I made my way through my day—drawing and painting the mural by the art room, working through the Phylum Chordata data in science class, trying not to cringe at every algebraic equation in math, discussing the historical implications of Ancient Greece, and reading through another round of English grammar—I kept coming back to my earlier fight with Ayah and Chelsea.

Well, not Chelsea, I thought, remembering how she had deflected Ayah's anger from me.

Chelsea has always been such a good defender.

I appreciated that so much more, knowing as I did that she'd had more than her share of trouble.

Chelsea had grown up in the Hartman family as the youngest of seven siblings, with her oldest brother more than thirteen years older than she was. When we were younger, we never spent much time at her house, because it was always full of wedding plans or baby showers or new jobs or birthdays. When I did go, between all the extended family and

124

friends, I felt like I needed four more ears and two more arms to juggle all the conversations and other people.

In many ways, I envied Chelsea for her large family; having no one to call my own, really, I always thought larger families were something of a comfort. A year before, when I asked Chelsea if she thought that, she snorted disdainfully.

"If they are," she told me, "mine is the exception that proves the rule."

"I thought you liked your family," I said.

"I do," Chelsea said. "But that doesn't mean we're comfortable. When everyone moves out and has a place of their own and we rent out the city convention center or the fire hall to have dinner, then we'll be comfortable."

"Well, I meant that it must be nice to have so many people to turn to if you need help," I said.

"That's what I have you, Jeff, and Reg for," Chelsea said. She rolled her eyes. "And Ayah, too, even though she'll probably make me get a makeover as payment."

I laughed. "She tries that on me, too," I said. "She'll grow out of it."

"Hopefully soon," Chelsea said. "I don't want to have to worry about that kind of stuff in junior high. I'm going to work hard so I can graduate early."

"Why?" I asked. I'd never thought of that. School always seemed to be a fixed sort of thing, and I never questioned it.

I'd already had quite a few "fixed-things" that had collapsed, so it never seemed like I would want more.

"It's just hard," Chelsea said. "Do you know how expensive college is? I'm the youngest, too, and even though Ginny didn't go to college, and Lou and Pepper aren't there yet, there's not going to be enough to cover us all."

"There are still a lot of ways to pay for college," I said, recalling how Rachel had plenty of ideas of how to pay for her schooling.

"Oh, I know. But that's not all of it," Chelsea said. "A lot of the others just don't care about me. Todd laughed when I said I wanted to be a computer engineer."

"That's because he's a dork," I said, thinking of Chelsea's second-oldest brother.

Chelsea grinned. "Well, that's true," she agreed. "But if you hear that you're stupid often enough, you'll begin to believe it. And that's what he says every time he comes home to visit."

"Didn't he just lose his job?" I asked.

Chelsea shrugged. "He says it's the economy."

"It could just as easily be incompetency," I argued, making her laugh again.

"But anyway, no," I insisted. "He's wrong. If he's saying you're dumb, he's got to be the stupidest person I know. You'd make a great computer engineer. You're always good

THE STARLIGHT CHRONICLES

at fixing my electronics, and I know Jeff's asked you for coding advice more than once on his Game Pac."

"Reggie's even needed me to help him with his glass cutter, too," Chelsea said.

"See? You're a genius, and all of us know it."

Chelsea grinned, and then we began talking about our science homework.

As we worked through our classwork, I made a promise to tell Chelsea she was a computer genius more often. It was the truth, really, but the truth is more powerful when you believe it.

After that conversation, I also decided it was best to stay away from the topic of her family. It came up from time to time on its own, but I never asked her to elaborate. Chelsea seemed to understand that I understood, and that was part of the reason we really were such great friends.

As I was walked away and turned down another hallway, it pained me to think I would need to find a way to distance myself even further from her. I'd known her for almost as long as I'd known Reggie.

I hoped I would not have to do anything drastic.

127

It was easy to avoid Ayah throughout the rest of the day. She was angry and upset and nothing good would come of us trying to talk to each other.

I wasn't sure anything good would come of us not talking, either, though.

In the end, I decided that if I had to give up my friends— and I did—then I would rather let the bonds between us break slowly. It would be more painful in the end, but I would willingly take on the pain if it meant I had a little more time with them.

Throughout Mrs. Akers' class, I managed to skirt around Chelsea, even though she tried to give me the math notes again. At her eager expression, I could only shake my head, and she backed down.

As she turned her attention to her own work, which was three or four chapters ahead of our current lesson, I had a feeling she was still confused about Ayah's reaction to me. *She might be a good defender, but that doesn't mean she won't play peacekeeper if she has to.*

After class, I allowed Mrs. Akers to keep me behind a few moments, patiently explaining x and y properties to me. Not only did she help me catch up on my lessons (just some, of course), but she let me find a way to be alone.

That was how the theory inside my mind went, anyway.

Walking down the empty halls, headed for my next class, I heard someone shout my name from behind me.

"Raiya!"

I glanced over my shoulder to see my other friend, Jeff Barns, as he headed over to me.

If I hadn't dedicated myself to losing my friends, I might have smiled. Jeff was tall and lanky, which made him stand out enough in different crowds, but everyone remembered him better because of his wild hair. His tawny curls flared out, bouncing as he hurried toward me.

While I waited for him, I thought about all the times he'd joked with Reggie about having an afro contest, to no avail—Reggie was content with his hair as it was, after all.

At the thought, the temptation to smile grew, but I determinedly squashed it down.

My power demanded that I control myself. That included my feelings.

"Hey, Jeff," I said.

"Raiya," he said, giving me his own beaming smile. "I haven't seen you since school started."

"That's not true," I huffed. "I was here the first week."

"Barely." He shoved his hands in the pants of his Rosemont uniform. "But I'm glad to see you now."

I eyed him suspiciously. "What do you need?" I asked.

He grinned. "You know me too well. I need you to come to the orchestra room. The harp needs tuned again."

A small sigh escaped me, and I couldn't tell if it was one of longing or irritation.

"I dropped out of orchestra this year," I finally said, realizing Jeff was waiting on me patiently.

"That's okay," he said. "But you know I'll still need to borrow you from time to time."

"Couldn't Chelsea help you with the harp?" I asked, as I turned and began walking with him. With each step I took, my resolve to protect my friends waned. It seemed I wanted their companionship, even if it meant trouble in the end, more desperately than I'd expected.

No, that wasn't true. I knew how much I wanted to keep them as friends. That was why I was depressed.

"Chelsea's better with the other strings," Jeff said. "That comes from playing the viola, for sure."

"But the harp is a string instrument," I pointed out.

"Yeah, well, it's one of the more obscure ones," Jeff said. "She even said that it would be better for you to do it, since you and that senior girl, Mandy, are the only ones who play it."

"Couldn't Mandy do it?" I grumbled. "I'm missing my next class."

"Come on, Raiya," Jeff goaded. "You've missed plenty of class. Why not another one?"

I nearly flinched at his kind reproach. "I guess you have a point," I reluctantly agreed. "But this is going to look bad on my record."

"I guess I have an advantage in that," Jeff said, as we entered the orchestra room. "I don't need to worry about my record too much."

"Why not?" I asked, as I walked up to the harp. It was an Ogden harp, a little over four feet in length. Since it was on a stand with wheels, it towered over me by a good six inches. I turned off the strings' levers, while Jeff fiddled with an electronic tuner.

"Well, Ayah's upset for a few more reasons than just what's between the two of you," he finally said. "I found out my dad's leaving."

"Leaving?" I turned around in disbelief.

Before that, Jeff's Soulfire had always reminded me of a melody—a small song, wrapped around inside of him, like music that was both made and being made.

As I looked at him, standing in the middle of the music room, surrounded by instruments and sheet music, I saw his soul had a new questing and testing element to it, one that was weighing carefully which way to go.

"Yeah," Jeff said. He lifted his blue-green eyes up to mine, and I could see they were full of unspoken sadness. "My parents are getting a divorce."

It is strange how so simple a sentence can complicate your life.

"Oh." I reached out and put my hand on his arm. "I'm so sorry."

He shrugged. "There's nothing you can do about it," he mumbled, and as much as I had a feeling that was true, it didn't mean that it was something I shouldn't mourn over.

When I told him as much, he sighed. And then I realized why Ayah was upset with him, too. "You decided to go with him, didn't you?" I asked.

"It's either that, or my mom is going back to Maine," Jeff said. He turned away from me. "I figured that if I go to Florida with my dad, I'll at least get out of dealing with the winter weather."

I squeezed his arm reassuringly, and immediately regretted it. A spurt of my power escaped, and I watched in horror as it hurried to settle into Jeff's heart.

I stepped back and stumbled as my foot bumped into the harp. Jeff grabbed me and steadied me, but the instant I had my balance back, I pulled away from him.

"You're upset, too?" Jeff asked, with a miserable look on his face.

Nothing happened to his Soulfire, I realized. I glanced down at my hands. Was something wrong? Was it not working anymore?

Carefully, I decided to test something. "When are you moving?" I asked.

He didn't seem to mind that I'd sidestepped his question. "When everything is settled," he said. "I'm not sure how long it will take, but it'll probably be in a few months. I know Dad wants to get out of here before winter. He's not too keen on them himself."

"I can understand that," I said. "Didn't you tell me that he only moved to Maine for your mom before?"

He nodded, and I nearly smacked myself—that wasn't really a great question to ask, if I was going to make him feel better.

Speaking of which ... I lightly placed my hand on his shoulder.

"I'm sorry," I said, this time apologizing for being insensitive as well as offering my condolences for his situation.

"It happens," Jeff said. He shrugged, and the second before my hand fell away from him, I released another bolt of my power. I watched as the supernatural power came and rested in his heart, and then it flickered away.

Nothing happened again.

I frowned. I would have to think about that, I decided. I thought about telling Grandpa Odd for a moment, before I decided not to. He would be upset that my power had affected Jeff to begin with, even though my instinct had been to comfort him.

I loved my grandfather, and as such, I hated disappointing him.

Before I could ask Jeff how he was feeling, he answered the question. "My parents had been fighting for a long time," he said. "So I'm a little relieved, to be honest. But I don't really want to move. When you know something is going to happen in the future like that, it really changes how you live in the moment."

Despite his ignorance of my destiny, Jeff's words offered me a gift—a moment where I didn't feel so alone. I mean, I felt bad for feeling that way; it's very selfish to be grateful for another person's pain. But the way he admitted how he felt, that his life was so focused on his future that everything became tainted by it, gave me unspeakable comfort.

I was also glad, shamefully, that I would not have to break our friendship. Jeff would go his way, and I would stay in Apollo City. Time would wean us away from each other, pulling us into different parts of our lives. If we ever did meet in the future, it would be as acquaintances more than friends.

Since that would be the case, I reached out and hugged him. He was quite a bit taller than me, but he hugged me back the way I imagined a big brother would. "Thank you," I said.

Thank you for being a good friend. Thank you for helping me keep a small part of my heart intact.

THE STARLIGHT CHRONICLES

"For what?" Jeff asked, as he stepped back from our embrace.

"For telling me," I told him, before giving him what I thought was a brave smile. "I know telling people things like that is not easy."

Of all people, I would know that, I thought bitterly. I had never revealed the truth regarding my secret.

"Well," I said carefully, "let me finish up with the harp here. So I can try to make my next class."

Jeff eagerly obliged me, and I was warmed by our conversation. In many ways, it felt like the beginning of a long a farewell. And maybe it was.

After I was done tuning the harp, Jeff grinned. "Thanks," he said. "Mandy's going to be glad, and so will all the orchestra teachers."

"No problem," I assured him.

"Well, I appreciate it anyways," he said.

"And I appreciate the distraction," I admitted, feeling safe enough to say that aloud.

Ayah's anger, and my supernatural concerns, had weighed heavily on me.

Jeff made me realize I didn't have to shut down. I could still do good things. I could still keep myself from falling apart.

It also helped I had a new puzzle to solve, too, considering I wondered why my power didn't help Jeff feel better.

"I know Ayah's upset," Jeff said. "But I did hear that she was going to visit Reggie in the hospital after school. Chelsea was going to go, too. I have to stay after to help with the band room stuff."

"Band room stuff?" I asked.

"They're getting a new influx of instruments, so a lot of these are going over to Apollo Central, along with the ones in the band room," he said, gesturing toward the plethora of instruments behind us. "Since I'm one of the bigger students, I'm going to stay and help load them."

"Good luck."

"Why don't you go with Ayah and Chelsea? That might help Ayah calm down some, if you go."

"I don't know," I said with a shrug. I decided not to mention I had an appointment with Dr. Dinger, and I would be at the hospital anyway.

"Well, you haven't seen him in a while either, right?" Jeff asked. "It might be good for you to go and see him, even if it's not with Ayah."

"You've got a point," I agreed neutrally.

"Don't let Ayah get you down," Jeff said. He gave me a friendly pat on the shoulder. "I know she's also more than a little jealous of you, considering how she feels about Reggie and everything."

136

I groaned. "Was I seriously the only person who didn't know he liked me?"

"Probably."

"It was a real shock," I admitted.

"Oh, I know you both very well, and I told him it was too early to say anything. Considering you both ended up going to the hospital, I'm pretty sure I was right."

"Yeah, no kidding." I grabbed my briefcase again. "I wonder why he started to like me anyway. He's not that old."

"Neither are you," Jeff reminded me.

I laughed, but inside I felt only weariness. I felt like I'd lived forever by the time junior high came around.

"Still," I said, "I don't know why he would change his mind."

"Well, lots of people from elementary school are starting to think about dating, too," Jeff remarked. "That's probably part of it. And the other part, well … "

"Well, what?"

"Give yourself some credit," Jeff said. "You're probably very easy to fall in love with, if you didn't insist on keeping your distance so much."

I wrinkled my nose. "Please."

"It's true," Jeff insisted.

"You remind me of Rachel when you say stuff like that," I said, making a face.

He grinned. "Well, it serves you right. Reggie talked to me for so many hours about how much he loved you, it's only fair I get to make you squirm some."

My face blanched, and Jeff's smile disappeared. "I'm sorry," he said. "I didn't mean to hurt you."

I swallowed the sudden lump in my throat. It was too hard to explain that I knew he was right, and I deserved it. "It's okay," I said. "But I think I'm going to check the harp one more time. So you can go on to your next class. There's no need to wait for me. Okay?"

Jeff seemed to take the hint that I wanted to be alone.

"Okay," he agreed. "I'll see you tomorrow."

I gave him a small smile, real enough that it didn't feel completely fake. "You know it. Bye."

He left, and I nearly wept with relief.

☼9☼
The Song of Light Inside of Me

After Jeff left me alone in the orchestra room, I gave up on going to my next class.

Instead, I did what I said I was going to do. I checked to make sure that the harp was properly tuned.

It wasn't as though I really thought I needed to; I just wanted to be alone again. I plucked one of the strings, listening to the pleasant *twang* that sang out. It made me realize how much I'd missed playing the harp and the violin lately. I loved classical music, and playing the violin always made me feel more like an instrument of beauty myself.

And as for the harp, I had a natural aptitude for it; it was something I knew, thanks to my paintings, that came from my previous life.

My fingers lit up in violet light, as I ran them through the strings again.

My heart eagerly joined in with the resounding notes, setting its usual slush and squeeze into a smoother rhythm. The melody carried me back to my own memories, and I thought more of those moments in my room, after I'd transformed, where I was confronted by the details of my former self.

It was true that Grandpa had told me of my origin. I was a Star—inside of me, my spirit combined my own Soulfire wrapped in Starfire, combined with Starsoul. Like a human, my heart, mind, and will were all represented by these

139

formations. There was just one difference. As a fallen Star, my spirit was dead, and I was unable to connect with the Celestial Kingdom.

Grandpa had told me that it made no matter; a dead spirit was just a ghost, and there was no reason to think it was dead and useless. I frowned as I thought of that. It was one of the more unusual things Grandpa taught me, but as my painting skills seemed to lend themselves to helping me recover my memory, I had no reason to doubt him.

My power brushed through the harp strings again. A familiar song started to play, as I stood there, remembering.

Grandpa had told me that I was a Guardian Star, the Star of Justice. I was born to be eternal, like the other Stars, and I was a defender of Earth.

Another image passed through my mind—the eyes I'd seen, reflected in the smoke down at the marina. I was supposed to protect it from creatures like him. Demons and monsters and minions and the unliving parasites that still required a host to survive in different realms.

That creature was one of the ones I was supposed to destroy. He was bound to the Void, bound inside of the Earth.

Just as my sisters had been imprisoned inside of me, I recalled.

My sisters—Maia, Asteropy, Alcyonë; Elektra, Meropae, Celaena, Taygetay.

THE STARLIGHT CHRONICLES

I saw my sisters, all of them glowing and happy, the Seven Starry Virtues who worked not only to keep the kingdom safe, but to make it continually more perfect, even as it was perfect already. Others were there, too, but I was unwilling to stay in my memory long enough to watch, knowing that I had destroyed them in the end.

I had destroyed myself in the end, too, I realized. I had used my wish—the power of a Star—to capture them again, to capture them and condemn them to the Void along with myself.

But they're not destroyed, I recalled. They were still free. They were the Sinisters now.

I had a new chance to capture them and send them to the void.

I glanced down, looking over myself. I was still in my regular form, but even though I was a shadow of my former Star self, I knew it was a miracle that I was even alive. There was no reason I should have been born into this realm and allowed to capture them again.

Grandpa said that was the reason I was here. I was here to right my mistake. I was here to correct what I had wronged, in order to earn my place back at Adonaias' side.

The harp's music enthralled me.

Another painting came to mind. It was the one where I'd been playing the harp with another Star, Orpheus, while in the sky beyond our light, another Star—or was it a Star at all?—watched.

The other Star captured my attention.

He was the same one, I recognized, as the one in the other painting. He was a corrupted Star who I was supposed to judge. He was to be a fallen Star, but for some reason, the Prince had stopped me.

I frowned. Why did Adonaias stop me?

And then all at once, I fell into the music, and I fell into myself.

I was back in that moment of my previous life, when I was the Star of Justice. I wore robes and armor of white, and I carried a sword with wings at the hilt by my side. For a moment, I fought down the urge to gasp, but found that I couldn't; I was trapped by the Immortal Realm's power, into acting as I had when I had actually been there.

"Star of Justice," Adonaias said. His voice was clear and kind, full of thunder and power and patience. I almost wept in hearing it again, so clearly. "Stop."

"What is it?" I asked.

"I must say you are right in your judgment. Yes, this Star, should he be called that, should die as a result of his actions. However, there is a higher calling you have forgotten."

"What?" I felt my face fall into an expression of incredible surprise. "My Lord, what do you mean? This Star has defiled your kingdom. He does not belong here. He has been tainted by Alküzor and his followers."

I glanced at the Star before me, the one that was on trial. His eyes were dull and black, already carrying a hollow void. His wings were gray and weathered, and I could feel the last of his eternal power as it drained out of him.

I was actually surprised that he was able to stay there at all.

But I wasn't surprised a moment later, when Adonaias shook his head. "Alküzor used his own power to twist shadows into the Star of Fire—"

"And this is the result?" I looked horrified at the creature before me. I looked closer to see the creature's face was deeply scarred and twisted.

But ... there was something familiar ...

"Yes. He has chosen a forbidden road, but—"

"How awful!" I whispered. The bound creature before me howled and moaned, a chilling sound. "We must destroy him at once then, if this is the case. His life is indeed an abomination to us."

"You are forgetting the higher standard, Astraiya," Adonaias reminded me firmly. "He has decided to come back to our side, of his own choosing."

"So? He has already chosen death," I murmured, frustrated. *Surely the Prince would not allow this contaminated slug of a creature to continue to exist.*

I didn't want to abandon my judgment; this thing did not deserve existence. But why would the Prince allow him to escape judgment? "Are you saying, Lord, that he deserves a chance to choose death again?" I asked carefully.

"No."

"Death is the proper sentence of a dead creature. Very well then, Lord," I said, looking back at the creature, trying hard not to cringe at the ugliness of the beast before me.

I was surprised when he caught my gaze.

I felt myself falter. "You, beast of the ashes, have committed crimes against the kingdom of the First Light. You have proven true to your choice."

"Yet I sense there is a small part of your heart," Adonaias said softly, interrupting me, "that remains willing to change."

The creature nodded, and Adonaias smiled.

"There are more things you long for, I see." At his words, the creature twisted around to face him.

I watched, half-horrified, as the Prince smiled kindly, reaching over and putting his hand on the beast's shoulder.

I did not know what to do. My Prince, touching the darkened skin of this thing, this horrible creature?

It was too much.

I was awed by the compassion of Adonaias as much as I was disgusted by the very thought of the creature. I waited for the Prince to move, but was only further surprised to see him reach into his robe and pull out the Light of Life.

"Today, you have been set free," Adonaias told the beast. "You have been given true light, and in that is life."

He poured the light out from his own heart and into the hands of the creature.

I nearly cried out, as the light burned away the ashes of the creature. I turned my eyes from the sight, unable to bear the full brightness of the Prince's power.

When I turned to look back at the beast, I gasped.

Nothing about him was the same.

His bonds had broken free, and shattered against the power of the First Light. The black holes of his eyes had been transformed into the fullest seas, his face made whole and beautiful, and his wings seemed to have been made over with fire, as the newly sprouted fiery-colored feathers shimmered brightly against the celestial sky. He cheered with Adonaias, and the two of them celebrated.

All while I just stared.

When he did look back over at me, for some reason, I froze. Not in disgust or terror, but rather fascination.

Adonaias turned back to me. "My Star of Justice, you have made the right choice today. My father would approve, as I do." He came over to me and took my hand in his. "You have witnessed the new birth of a Star. However, it is not enough that he should be made new. He should be nurtured into his new life by someone who lights up the kingdom with love and justice. That is why I ask you to watch over him and be his friend. Here, take his hand."

I felt the warm of the Star's fingers as he reached out and took my hand. Something stirred within me uncontrollably as I looked up into his face.

He looked so much like the Prince, radiantly beautiful and humble. He reached out with his other hand and encased my hand in his completely. "Thank you, Lady Justice, for allowing me to live," he said, his first new smile flitting to his face.

I felt myself look over at Adonaias, who merely smiled that enigmatic smile of his own back at me.

"He is in need of a name, Lord," I said softly.

Adonaias nodded. "What do you think we should name him?"

"We?" I was briefly taken aback. The way the Prince had said that, it was almost like this Star was for me …

"My Lady?" The Star turned to me expectantly.

My fingers tingled underneath his hands, and I smiled despite herself. I looked back over at Adonaias, who was waiting patiently for my response. "Almeisan," she said. "His name is Almeisan."

"Very fitting," Adonaias agreed. He reached out and placed his one hand on my shoulder, and his other on Almeisan's. "Almeisan, welcome to our family."

"Thank you, Adonaias." Almeisan bowed. When he looked up again, there was a charming smile on his face. "And thank you, too, Lady Justice."

"Astraiya," I said. "You may call me Astraiya."

His eyes lit up even more wondrously. "Astraiya," he said, as though he was savoring the way that my name sounded on his tongue. "Thank you."

There was a strange stirring in my heart as I accepted his thanks. In my otherworldly awareness, I realized that my heart, though whole, was suddenly fuller and more empty. There was a new song that was suddenly born inside of me, as my own inner light burned for him.

I felt Almeisan's hand tighten around mine, and Adonaias smiled. "It is good," he said, "for justice to be tempered by mercy. Take good care of him, Lady Justice."

The school bell rang, a trillion and a half light-years and millions of moments away, summoning me back to the Moral

Realm and all its temporal strangeness. The song stopped, and as I opened my eyes, I was not surprised to find them wet with unshed tears.

The music had stopped, but the rhythm of life carried on. I heard the crowded hallway outside the music room.

"I failed," I whispered, remembering the bright red feather in my hair that appeared when I transformed. Almeisan had been destroyed.

That was the only explanation, I thought. What else would I deserve, but to lose him as well as Adonaias?

I would need a miracle, I thought, to get back to both of them.

Or maybe a wish.

"Would that even work?" I wondered. I didn't know. I thought about my own mission, to protect Earth. I would have to protect it from the Sinisters. Maybe if I captured them again, I would be reinstated.

Would that work, Adonaias?

There was no answer. But I decided to keep the thought in mind and mull over it some more. It would not hurt to ask, and get a definite answer.

I sighed. I would have to consider the matter later. The next period was starting soon.

That was when I realized someone—or something—was in the room with me.

A faint whisper called from behind me, and I felt a sudden twinge of pain in my wrist.

"*Yashool.*"

I straightened at once, whirling around. Something caught at the corner of my vision. It was a shadow.

My mouth went dry. *Could it be … ?*

I frowned. I didn't think it was Alküzor. I knew he was bound inside the void, and he wouldn't be bothering me. He had no power in this Realm, even if his agents did.

So, who was the shadow then?

It couldn't be … I felt my breath squeeze out of me. *Could it be … him?*

"Almeisan?" I whispered softly. "Is that you?"

It shifted around in the air, keeping only a second ahead of my sigh. The ghostly howl cried out more softly this time. "*Yashool!*"

And then, all of a sudden, it attacked me. The ghastly body ran right through me, washing me in a wave of cold air. My energy dulled and I felt winded.

Before I could call on my power to retaliate, it left.

"*Yashool,*" the shadow howled, hurrying through the music room wall. I let myself sink to the floor, clutching at my heart, as despair overtook me.

☼10☼
Remittance for My Mistake

After seeing the shadow, and fearing that it was indeed the ghost of my former beloved, I was hungry for human companionship, so much so I was almost relieved to be heading for the hospital.

My certainty waned on the way over; I doubted I was prepared to see my friends. Ayah, Chelsea, and Reggie each gave me a reason to want to turn around and go back home, forget about my appointment, curl up in my bed, and talk to Grandpa about homeschooling.

Of all of them, Ayah had the worst temper. One time in fifth grade, a few months after she'd moved to Apollo City, she yelled at a boy who splashed paint on her new dress during art class. It was an accident, but the boy still ended up crying and the art teacher had to call the principal.

The thought of seeing Chelsea again made my knees feel weak. I hated the thought of her in pain, considering how much she had already faced from her family, and I hated the idea of losing her respect. She had been a teacher to me in so many ways besides math, and a friend to me in some of my darkest moments.

And Reggie … Seeing him in his coma, knowing I was responsible for putting him there, making his family worry, ruining his life, and breaking his heart …

I looked down at my hands, my expression unspeakably grim.

"I'm just *trying* to make this difficult for myself, aren't I?" I murmured to myself, as I walked into the hospital.

Looking back on it later, I would both laugh and cry at my innocence; little did I know, there were even more difficult things ahead of me.

I had a follow-up appointment with Dr. Dinger, but I decided to take the long route past Reggie's room. I figured that would be the best way for me to see him, if I could see him at all, and see if my other friends were there, too.

I caught sight of Reggie's room. His parents were out in the hallway, just a little way down from his door.

My steps faltered as doubt clouded my resolve. I wasn't sure that they would let me see him, and, after saving Reggie's dad only days before, I worried—probably needlessly—that he would recognize me from the marina fire.

It didn't help that next to them, I saw the pregnant, professional-looking woman carrying an oddly ominous stack of papers in her hand. Realizing she was a lawyer, I stopped completely.

Every lawyer has a little intimidation built into their profession, almost as if it's an invisible part of their wardrobe. This is especially true when you grow up remembering visits from them, discussing everything from social workers to family wills. I had to give this lady lawyer props; she managed to intimidate me, drastically, from just looking at her.

She was a little on the short side, but she wore the heels to make up for it. Her hair was sleek and tied back, and her clothes were pressed and smooth enough there was only a small, distinct shadow of a baby belly showing. If it wasn't for the way she was carrying her papers, my eyes might have passed over that fact completely.

When I noticed it, there was no more ignoring it.

Especially since I noticed she was having contractions, and she was trying to hide it, and *that* really made me terrified. She was in the middle of a meeting, prepared to carry it out to the end, and she was in the beginning stages of labor.

"Well," I muttered, "that's dedication."

I watched as she breathed in quick, shallow breaths, as she talked to Kaya, Reggie's mom. I could tell Kaya was uncomfortable, but neither of them seemed willing to stop her.

Since they were trapped in what I could tell was an important meeting, I made a quick calculation and slithered into Reggie's room.

Immediately, I almost wished I hadn't.

Reggie was hooked up to several machines. Even after all my own time in the hospital, I didn't know what all of them were for. His hair was still twisted into his favorite dreadlocks, and it seemed as though they'd gotten a lot longer.

"Hi, Reggie," I murmured, reminding myself how much I needed to control myself. I felt like crying, but I pushed it back. I had to keep my focus, I told myself.

I walked up to him, breathing in and out several times before I talked to him.

"I hope you're feeling better," I whispered. "I'm sorry for what happened. I'm not even entirely sure what exactly happened, even though I know I broke your heart."

My eyes turned toward his heart monitor. It beeped steadily, if slowly, and I welcomed the rhythm.

"You should know Ms. Carmichael's managed to keep Courtney from our mural," I said, my mouth feeling dry. "I didn't really do a lot of work on it in the past couple of weeks since … since you left."

There was still no response.

Carefully, I reached out and took his hand. "I don't really want to work on it without you," I admitted. "But it's better I do it than Courtney gets a hold of it, right?" My small attempt at a joke gave me nothing.

I glanced back at the doorway. I didn't hear anyone coming; there was the usual scatter of background noise I'd become familiar with at Apollo City Hospital—the loudspeaker system frizzles, the walkie-talkie buzzes, the movements of stretchers and gunneries and other machines, the alternative flurry and flutter of feet along the hallway floors.

Looking back at Reggie, missing the light from his eyes, I decided that I had a chance to save him, and I was duty-bound to try.

153

THE STARLIGHT CHRONICLES

I put down my briefcase on the floor beside me and straightened my shoulders.

"Reggie," I said. "I can't tell you how much you have added to my life. I'm sorry that I can't love you the way you loved me."

I squeezed his hand, calling forth my power. "But I know you don't deserve to be stuck here, in the hospital, because of something I did."

My hands lit up with my heart's energy; in the darkened hospital room, I felt the world suddenly shift once more. Just like before, in the orchestra room, I was in a world of contrasting balances. There was dark and light, there was hope and hopelessness, and there was time and eternity, and all the worlds and wonders between.

I had the power to choose which way to empower.

"I choose to help you," I whispered. "I choose to do my duty, to honor our friendship. I choose to set you free from your pain."

Light poured out over him, filling the room and penetrating his skin. Emboldened by my dedication, I poured out everything I had into healing him.

Reggie's heart rate began to beat more quickly, as I gave everything I had to heal him.

A moment later, I frowned. Even though his heart was beating more quickly, nothing was happening. I narrowed my eyes, and I saw his Soulfire was the same as it had been last time—collapsed with despair, stagnant and still.

What's wrong? I wondered. *Why isn't he waking up? Why isn't his heart working right?*

I pushed even more of myself out of me. "Work," I ordered, not sure if I was talking to myself or praying that Adonaias would release Reggie from whatever ill had overcome him.

My energy was fading. I allowed my power to remain constant, despite my better judgment.

I have to save him. I have to.

I will save him, no matter the cost.

The light around me began to dull and swirl around. My knees were shaking. I grabbed Reggie's hand even more tightly, trying to ensure that he would be healed.

"What's wrong?" I whispered, angry and tired and frustrated beyond anything I'd ever felt before. "I managed to do this to him, why can't I fix it?"

My hand dropped from his, and I fell to my knees beside his bed.

I felt my vision blur a little, as my mouth went slack. I watched my power bubble around Reggie some more, whirling around into a vortex of sorts, before it slammed into him, hitting him right in his heart.

His body jolted some, and my heart filled with hope.

THE STARLIGHT CHRONICLES

"Reggie?" I called.

I was waiting for a response when I heard the footsteps behind me.

"What do you think you're doing?" A voice gasped behind me.

I was still slumped over on my knees, but at the voice, I jerked around.

The lawyer I'd seen was standing in the doorway to Reggie's room. She had a hand protectively wrapped around her pregnant belly, while her papers were slowly dropping from her other arm.

My power dispersed quickly, but it was too late. She'd seen it.

I said nothing as I looked at her; I was just staring at her, and she was just staring at me, all while I could see she was still struggling with her contractions.

Before I could say anything—or even think of anything to say, really—I saw Kaya and Tomas glance in behind her.

And then I saw Ayah and Chelsea peeking through the doorway behind them.

"It's a party," I heard myself say, and I wondered at just how weak I was, to be unable to stop myself from thinking aloud.

"Raiya?" Kaya asked.

"Hi, Mrs. Banks," I replied, hurriedly standing up and brushing myself off. "I was, um, just here to—"

"What did you do?" The lawyer came up beside me, where the heart monitor was beeping more strongly.

"Nothing," I lied. "I was just here to see Reggie."

"That's a lie," she snapped. "I saw something." She turned back to Reggie's parents. "She did something."

Ayah spoke up. "She said she did something before, too."

I glared at Ayah, suddenly angry. I knew she was Reggie's friend, and she was worried for him, but she was my friend, too, wasn't she? There was no reason that she had to make comments about things she didn't know about, especially when they were only going to make me get into more trouble.

"Are you okay?" Chelsea asked, speaking up for the first time.

"She did something," the lawyer said again, and I felt a renewed sense of terror, being on the disapproving end of her stare. "I saw it."

"What did you see, Cheryl?" Kaya asked, taking the calm, motherly type of method.

"There was a lot of light," she replied. "There was a huge cloud of it. And then when I saw her and said something, it went away."

Kaya and Tomas exchanged glances, while Ayah scowled at me, and Chelsea frowned, trying to make sense of what Cheryl was saying.

"I have no idea what you're talking about," I lied again as I reached for my briefcase. "Now, if you'll excuse me, I have an appointment."

"You shouldn't leave," Cheryl said, as a nurse came in behind her and began to check over Reggie's monitors. "You might have done something to him."

"She told me she did earlier," Ayah spoke up once more, and soon Cheryl and Ayah were in a deep conversation I wanted no part of.

I walked by Kaya and Tomas, trying not to feel bad for them. I had hoped to get Reggie back, for my own benefit, for my own duty. But as much as I grieved for him, I knew my own feelings in the matter were only a drop compared to what his parents had to be feeling.

Kaya nodded kindly to me. "I'm sure you did nothing wrong, Raiya," she said as I walked past. "Thank you for coming. But next time, please check in with the nurse station. It's policy here."

I nodded. My hands tightened around my briefcase. "Thank you," I said. "It's nice to see you again, Mrs. Banks."

She gave me a tight smile, and I could see she was stressed. I looked over at Reggie's dad, and saw he was deeply concerned, too.

THE STARLIGHT CHRONICLES

"I'm glad to see you're feeling better, too, Mr. Banks," I said. "I, uh, read about what happened in the paper."

Reggie's dad shrugged. "I'm okay," he said. "I would feel better if Reggie was doing better."

"I understand," I assured him.

Before I could make my escape to Dr. Dinger's floor, Cheryl called out from behind me. "Stop her from leaving," Cheryl said. "I want to ask her some questions."

"Cheryl, I'm sure it was nothing. Reggie's the same as he was before." Kaya gestured toward the heart monitor, close to where the nurse was adjusting his IV bag.

I looked over at Cheryl, watching as she took a deep, sharp breath in, and carefully exhaled in a practiced rhythm. Yep, I thought. She was definitely in labor.

"Maybe you would feel better if you sat down for a while," Reggie's dad said, patting Cheryl's arm. "Come on. Let's go find you a doctor."

"I'm only eight months pregnant," Cheryl insisted. "He's just rowdy today. We have business to attend to, and I will not be deterred ... "

I scooted out the door as Kaya and Tomas once more began to try to coax Cheryl to calm down. Before I could get very far, Ayah called out to me.

"Raiya!"

I groaned. "What?" I snapped, already tired and frustrated. I had been hoping so hard that Reggie would wake up, that I would be able to see the goodness in his eyes once more. Ayah's self-righteous indifference with Cheryl made me even more upset on top of everything else.

"What did you do?" Ayah asked, crossing her arms. "That lady said you did something, and you already told me earlier that you did something before."

"That lady's going into labor," I shot back. "She's hardly a credible source on the matter."

"But you said earlier—"

"It doesn't matter what I said earlier," I insisted. "I can't do anything to help him, and I just wanted to go and see him, alright? That's not a crime."

"It is against the rules of the hospital," Chelsea pointed out, and at her remark, I turned on her as well.

"Well, that doesn't matter either," I asserted. "I'm leaving now. I don't want to talk to you anymore. Either of you. And if you are worried that I did something to Reggie, maybe you better just stay away from me."

"That's not what I meant," Chelsea said, but I pushed past her.

"Well, that's what I mean," I insisted. I narrowed my eyes. "After all, Reggie ended up in the hospital because he asked me out on a date, and I didn't want to go on one. Our friendship is ruined now, and so maybe he's lucky he's in the hospital. Maybe he got what he deserved."

"He did not!" Ayah insisted. "Reggie's the kindest person we know, Raiya. That's a terrible, ugly thing to say. I can't believe you."

"Well, maybe you should find a better friend," I shot back. "I don't think I want to be a friend to someone who's willing to turn me over to a lawyer at the least provocation."

"I wouldn't call this the *least* provocation," Chelsea tried again. "And you have to admit, Raiya, you don't like to talk to us about these things. When you do, you always give us vague answers."

"We have a right to protect Reggie from you," Ayah added. "Even if he's not your friend, he's ours, and we will make sure that he is safe."

"Good," I said, my voice dripping with disdain. "And good job so far. I'll leave you to protect him some more right now."

"Good."

"*Good.*" I gave them one last dirty look, and then twisted away from them.

I thought I saw the shadow of the demon again—Yashool, as I called him—but I was too tired to care. I ignored him as I left Reggie's hospital wing.

My heart was sore as I hurried up the stairs. My head throbbed in pain. I was tired. I was angry. I was upset. I was alone.

But my friends were free. Reggie was beyond my help. Chelsea and Ayah were cut off from me. Jeff was moving away soon.

They were free.

I was free.

I was free, and I was more miserable than I had ever been. I barely realized that someone was holding me while I cried. It was only when Dr. Dinger said my name that I looked up and saw him.

☼11☼
The Doctor and the Lawyer

"Oh. Dr. Dinger." I blinked and blushed, hurriedly wiping my tears away as I glanced up at him.

I'd come running into his office, upset and overwhelmed, and flung myself into his arms before either of us had really registered what was going on. I shuffled out of his arms quickly, trying to fight my growing embarrassment. "I'm sorry," I apologized.

He shook his head. "It's alright," he told me. "Everything will be okay."

His assertion might as well have been a sledgehammer to my already broken heart.

"How do you know?" I whispered.

"I tell my son the same thing," he said. "And we've managed to hang in there so far."

"I hope the day will never come when you won't be able to tell him that, then," I said curtly.

"Me, too." Dr. Dinger took my shoulders. "But let's not worry about him. I'm sure that Hamilton would be upset if he knew I was talking about him anyway."

I nodded, having no real response to that.

"What are you upset about?" Dr. Dinger asked. "Is it a boy?"

"What?" I nearly gagged. "No."

He gave me a smile. "I thought I'd ask. You're in junior high now, and it seems like all the kids are dating younger and younger these days."

"I don't even know why," I said. "I don't want to date anyone. I don't want my friends to change."

"Unfortunately, that's not up to us," Dr. Dinger said. He pulled out my file from his pile on his desk. "But let's head to an exam room, alright? Is your grandpa coming soon?"

I shrugged. "He's supposed to be here," I said. "He's pretty good about getting here on time."

"Well, we still have a little bit of time," Dr. Dinger said, pointing to the clock on the wall. I still had five minutes until my appointment.

"Can I ask you a question, without him around?" I asked, suddenly curious.

"Sure. Patient-doctor confidentially applies unless you give the word."

"Alright. Then I have a question," I said.

"What is it?" Dr. Dinger asked patiently.

I sighed. "Well, I was wondering ... do you think there will ever be a day when my heart is normal?"

I already knew the answer. But I wanted to know what he thought.

THE STARLIGHT CHRONICLES

I could tell from his expression that he hadn't been expecting that question.

"I don't know," he said. "I think your best bet is to get a new heart."

I might as well wish for a new wish, I thought. I nodded slowly.

"I will say, I don't think it helps you any to stress out about it."

"What do you mean?" I asked.

"You're young," he said. "You have time. You might as well enjoy it. Hang out with your friends, try to relax. Don't overexert yourself. I think that's where a lot of these panic attacks are coming from."

His response made sense, even if none of it was possible.

"I know," he continued, "that school can be stressful. But surely there are some things about it you enjoy?"

I nodded again. "I like my art class," I said.

"Maybe there's more you can do with it, then," he suggested. "I know you go to Rosemont. Maybe you can find an afterschool activity to help with that would allow you to work with the art department more?"

Nothing came to my mind, but I promised I would think about it.

"Good," he said. "Try to find something that makes you happy, Raiya."

"Happiness is fleeting and a result of what happens to you," I said, remembering what Grandpa had told me once about it.

"Happiness is probably not the best description then," Dr. Dinger said. "Maybe I meant more like joy. Find something that gives you joy, and then cling to that as much as you can."

"As much as I can," I mumbled, thinking of how much my Starlight power limited me in that regard. Still, his advice was sound.

I looked back up at him. "Do you think I'm going to die?" I asked.

Again, he was surprised by my question. But this time, he surprised me by his answer.

"I hope not," he said. "You're a strong, lovely young lady with her whole life ahead of her. You obviously want to make the world a better place. I know I would be among the least of people who would be terribly sad if something happened to you."

He opened the door to an exam room for me, holding it politely as I headed in.

"You won't … you won't tell my grandpa that I came in here crying, will you?" I asked, suddenly worried. I didn't want Grandpa to think I was going crazy or soft or anything. I mean, I was really disappointing him enough at this point. I'd been careless with Jeff, and downright defiant when it came to trying to heal Reggie.

Dr. Dinger shook his head. "There's no need for me to tell him, unless you want me to," he said. "That's up to you."

"I'd rather keep that private," I said. "If you don't mind."

"I don't mind at all," he assured me, and I knew I was right to trust him.

Before I could thank him for all his kindness, a small *beep* went off, and I recognized it as an alert.

"What's that?" I asked, glad for the diversion. I appreciated Dr. Dinger, but I was getting tired of making a fool of myself in front of him. The small beeper went off again, and I knew it had been the same one that I'd heard before, at my last appointment.

He took out a small device, one I didn't recognize. "They don't recommend I carry my phone," he explained, "since they can cause a lot of distractions and sometimes they can interrupt different machines here in the cardio care ward. So I have this alert signal, which lets me know I'm supposed to contact my wife."

"Oh." *I guess that makes sense,* I thought.

"So if you'll excuse me," he said, "I'll go and see what she needs, and then, hopefully when I get back, your grandpa will be here and we can take care of your check-up."

I nodded. "Okay. Thanks."

I watched as he headed out the door, back down toward his office. And then I was all alone again. I was grateful to be alone again—I was very, very tired, and from using my power as much as I had earlier, I was ready to take a nap.

I was just giving the idea serious consideration when I saw Dr. Dinger hurrying back down the hallway, a frightened look on his face.

I jumped off the cot and leaned out the door. "What is it, doctor?" I asked.

He jumped as he saw me. "Raiya," he said. "I'm sorry, but I'm going to have to reschedule your appointment. I have to go tend to some family matters. Go ahead and check in with my assistant for another time. I don't see him right now, but he should be up here in a few moments."

"Oh."

I was surprised by the rush of disappointment. But, I had to admit, the thought of going home, going to bed, and forgetting all the terribleness of the day, was extremely tempting.

Dr. Dinger didn't wait for me to answer. He sped on down the hall.

Curiosity suddenly struck me, and I looked for a glimpse of his Soulfire. As he ran, I narrowed my eyes and allowed myself a quick glimpse at his Soulfire. It wasn't spying, I thought. I was just checking on his well-being. It was largely the same thing as checking a temperature or taking a pulse.

I was not expecting abnormal results. As I looked on it, his Soulfire made me frown; the familiar, bright light I knew was suddenly cloaked in fear.

"Dr. Dinger?" I called out. "What's wrong?"

He didn't hear me. Or if he did, he didn't answer.

I was horrified to see that he was afraid—more afraid than I'd ever known was possible for him. He was, after all, a man who dealt with life and death and all their minute details on a daily basis. What did he have to be afraid of?

Maybe it's a demon monster, I thought. I thought of the one I'd seen hanging over Ayah and Chelsea, and the one I'd seen in the orchestra room earlier in the day.

Was it possible they had come for me?

It was too dangerous of a question to leave it unanswered. So, trying to muster up my energy, I hurried after him.

I kept far enough behind Dr. Dinger that, if I did see something and needed to transform, I would be out of sight and safe.

I only hesitated for the briefest second, when I saw him exit the stairs at Reggie's floor.

What if I'd hurt Reggie even more? What if Dr. Dinger has been called in because Reggie's dying?

Knowing that Dr. Dinger was not in charge of Reggie was the *only* thing that allowed me to walk through the door after him.

169

But when I slipped through the door, I saw that Dr. Dinger was helping shift Cheryl, the pregnant lawyer, into a wheelchair.

I was petty enough to enjoy a moment where Cheryl was no longer intimidating. Given our prior discussion, I thought it was appropriate, even if it wasn't kind.

"Come on, Mark, I need to go over the papers just a little bit more!" Cheryl let out a distorted grunt as another contraction.

"Why did you call me then, Cheryl?" Dr. Dinger asked, keeping his tone light. From the way he said it, I wondered if he was having a hard time not smiling.

I was not the only one who sensed that, apparently, because Cheryl grabbed his wrist. "Consider yourself lucky I'm in a horrendous amount of pain," she snapped, "or I would draw up the divorce papers."

It was at that moment I realized that Cheryl was his wife. It was quite a surprise, to say the least; I'd always imagined Dr. Dinger's wife as someone who radiated warmth and compassion. Needless to say, the five minutes I'd spent in Cheryl's presence earlier did not lend that impression.

Transfixed, I watched as Dr. Dinger knelt down next to her. Shamelessly, I inched forward.

"Ah, Cheryl, my love," he whispered. "After all these years, you never fail to make me love you more."

"I could kill you with my bare hands right now, you know."

170

Dr. Dinger gave her a quick kiss on the forehead. "I know you're frightened," he said. "He's early, I know. But everything will be alright. You'll see."

"You don't know that," Cheryl insisted, her teeth grinding together. She was trying to hold back from crying out, as another contraction lashed through her.

"If you would please help me get her down to the maternity ward," Dr. Dinger said, handing Cheryl's stack of papers to Kaya, "I would greatly appreciate it."

Reggie's dad quickly took over pushing the wheelchair. "We can definitely help, doctor." He gave Cheryl a kind smile. "We can wait on the fine print, too."

Cheryl tried to reply, as they walked down the hallway, toward the elevators. From where I was hiding, I could see Reggie's parents following; I had to wonder if Cheryl was calling out to them, still going over their paperwork.

I came out from behind the door just as Dr. Dinger glanced back in my direction. "Go back upstairs to my office, Raiya," he called to me, and the adrenaline rush, the one I'd felt at seeing Dr. Dinger so terrified, slowed. I felt myself jolt uncomfortably, as my energy was nearly gone.

I glanced around again, seeing if my friends—or my ex-friends—were there still, too. Fortunately for me, Ayah and Chelsea were nowhere to be seen.

Briefly, I toyed with the idea of going back in to see how Reggie was doing, but I decided against it. It was too hard to imagine being able to do anything else for him, especially since I was already weary from before.

As much as I'd hurried after my doctor, I found myself sluggishly making my way up to his office once more. My footsteps dragged out; each step was like a pounding drum.

I smiled for a brief moment, thinking of Jeff and his many bands. They would be appalled by my rhythm here, I thought, chagrined.

Despite my slowness, my wavering vision, and my wayward steps, no one seemed to notice me as I made my way to Dr. Dinger's office once more. I knew I had to reschedule our appointment, and I decided to do it quickly so I could go home and rest.

I was supposed to wait for his assistant, so I slumped over in the small patient chair. Immediately, I decided that his high back swirl chair would let me sleep more easily, and I was okay with falling asleep while I waited.

It was impossible for me not to want to sleep at that point. I tried calling up my power, just to see if I could use it, and nothing happened. I was drained, and too tired to really care that I had no reserve left in me.

I flopped into his chair. The wheels fluttered back at my impact, and I hit the cabinet behind me. A shuffle of files fell down, and I groaned.

"Ugh. I suppose I better pick them up."

THE STARLIGHT CHRONICLES

It was an extremely charitable move on my part. I rubbed my eyes and focused as much as I could. When I realized there were several papers from different files that had fallen, I put the different papers in a stack, hoping that Dr. Dinger would forgive me for the trouble.

"Well, it's not like he doesn't have something more important to worry about right now," I recalled, thinking of Cheryl and her pregnant belly.

She had been having contractions pretty badly when I saw her earlier, I thought. Was it possible she was going to have her baby today?

Before I could wonder too much about that, I caught sight of my name on the papers.

I glanced over it; if it had my name on it, I had a right to know, right? I glanced down at it, and instantly regretted skipping so much of my biology class.

"'Specimen samples will be arranged for pickup at the discretion of the recipient?'" I frowned. What were they talking about? "'Testing results will be shared at the discretion of the processor?'"

I read enough to know I didn't have any idea of what it was for. The data I was able to understand contained many vague details.

I glanced down at the back of the sheet. I was surprised to see Grandpa's signature. Below that, it had the logo for the Skarmastad Foundation, and Ogden Skarmastad's patented signature as well.

173

Briefly, I noticed similar strokes of the two signatures. After a moment of study, I shook my head. "For all Grandpa wants to distance himself from his Skarmastad relatives, he sure seems to write like they do."

I glanced at the rest of the papers, but I was still tired. I finally decided to let it go. There was nothing I could do, right?

I just put them back in a neat stack when I saw the last one on the floor underneath the desk.

I picked the paper up. And then I stared at it, blinking several times to make sure I was reading it correctly.

"'Subjects injected with serum from Specimen showed immediate signs of improvement, suggesting a significant resistance to cellular decomposition and disease. More testing will be required. More blood samples needed.'" I read through the list, amazed to see what the Specimen—me— had been able to do for the people suffering.

Remembering the needles that would poke my arm for each drawing, I flinched. Was Dr. Dinger trying to get my blood for a research project?

The thought angered me at first, that he would do this without my permission or without telling me. I was further upset to realize that Dr. Dinger was inadvertently putting me and Grandpa in danger. I did not want anyone, people or demons alike, to come after me for my blood.

Then I had a thought.

Maybe ... maybe my blood would be able to heal Reggie. It worked miracles for other people, apparently. Why not him?

I decided to go and see Dr. Dinger. After I asked him why the Skarmastad Foundation wanted more of my blood, I would see what else he knew; Grandpa had told me that they were the ones whose charity paid for my appointments with Dr. Dinger in the first place, but this seemed too strange and secretive for it to be unimportant.

After I got my answers, I would make him get me back into Reggie's room. If my blood was able to heal people specifically, I would not allow Reggie to suffer.

☼12☼
The Blood of a Star

One of the better tricks that I learned when I was young was how to be invisible.

Not literally invisible, but the kind of invisible where you go unnoticed by other people, even if you walk right by them.

The trick was to believe as though you were of no importance, to believe that you had nothing to do with anyone else's life, so you could walk through as easily as if you were a ghost of sorts. People always seemed to play along with this when I would slump my shoulders forward, tuck my chin down by my chest, and let my bangs fall over my eyes.

And today is no exception, I thought, only half-bitter, as I made my way to the maternity ward. Catching sight of "Cheryl Thomas-Dinger" on one of the room charts, I headed further down the hallway.

The nurses were running around, and as they passed me, with no concern for who I was or why I was there, I realized that I was sensing something again.

Glancing around, I wondered if that demon from before, the one I had seen hanging over my friends, had followed me down here.

I stopped as a chill went through me.

"Or worse," I whispered. "He could be doing something here."

Panic set in, and I used it to power myself to find Dr. Dinger and his wife. They were in trouble.

They had to be. Why else would I feel this way?

I walked by Cheryl's room and I heard her screaming. Not in pain, but in fear.

"What's wrong?" she cried. "What's wrong with him? You can do something, can't you?"

The baby.

I felt my mouth dry as tears came welling up into my eyes. She was losing the baby.

As the nurses and Dr. Dinger tried to console her, tried to list out options, I sneaked into the room.

There was a small, premature baby lying down in one of the hospital's plastic bassinets.

I watched as Cheryl began to panic more, trying to throw herself around, trying to break free from the nurses who were cleaning her up.

She eventually stilled, as Dr. Dinger held her. She was crying, and he was holding onto her. There were other nurses trying to console her as well.

I walked over to the baby myself. He had a pink, squishy face. He wasn't moving much, like I would expect a newborn to do, anyway. I remembered that Cheryl had said she was only eight months pregnant.

"Prep the baby for emergency care," one of the nurses said. "Arrange an immediate transfer to the NICU."

I reached out and took a hold of the baby's hand, letting his tiny fingers wrap around mine.

"What are you doing in here?" One the nurses finally caught sight of me standing there. I glanced over my shoulder, only to find myself face-to-face with a stern-faced midwife.

Before I could answer, and answer with something that didn't involve anything supernatural, Dr. Dinger called to me.

"Raiya, what are you doing here?" Dr. Dinger's voice was full of surprise. He glanced down at the baby, who still held onto me, and saw that he was moving and breathing normally; then he turned back to me.

As his eyes met mine, a whole unspoken conversation seemed to take place between us.

"The baby is anemic," the nurse called out. "His heart rate is low and falling. We will need a blood transfusion."

"I can help," I said.

"You will?" Dr. Dinger asked. I could tell he was anxious and unsure, but he wasn't willing to discard my assistance.

Another midwife came up beside me. "Doctor, we need to get him transferred to the NICU, stat," she said. She turned to me and said, "You shouldn't be here, little girl."

"She can stay," Dr. Dinger said. He watched as they began to hook his new son up to different devices.

"Doctor, you know as well as I do this is against protocol."

"I will call security," another nurse declared. "A baby's life is in danger, and we can't have shenanigans going on like this."

"No." Dr. Dinger stepped in front of me.

"Mark, for God's sake, listen to him!" Cheryl barked. She was still in tears. "They need to save our baby!"

"Excuse us, nurse," Dr. Dinger said, his voice tense and tight. "Please see to Cheryl. Take her to her room and we will follow shortly."

Cheryl had likely never been told no in all her career. "But—"

"But what about … " The nurse glanced over to me.

"She is my patient," Dr. Dinger said. He clapped a hand on her shoulder. "I'll take care of her."

The nurse shook her head. "This is a mistake," she huffed, but she did what he asked.

Cheryl caught sight of me and screamed. "No! Don't let that girl near my baby," she cried, as she was moved from the birthing bed into a wheelchair. "Stop! Stop moving me."

But Dr. Dinger shut the door after her. "Alright, Raiya. He's premature, anemic, and his heart is failing."

"I can help," I assured him. I paused for a short second before asking, "You know I can, don't you?"

"Yes." The line of his jaw was tight.

"I saw the research papers in your office," I said, trying to remember why I had come down here in the first place.

"Yes," Dr. Dinger said. "Please, we can talk about it later. Please just save my son first."

I was still tired, as I called on my power. "I just need a few moments," I said, stifling down a yawn as I picked up the baby. I cradled him against me, letting myself feel his heart beat against my own. None of my Starlight power stirred inside of me, but I could hear my heart hum, delighted with the little guy even as I was sorry for his pain.

"Sit down," Dr. Dinger said. "You look exhausted."

"I went to see Reggie earlier," I half-heartedly explained, as I did as he said. The small chair was unusually comfortable, and my feet were relieved to have a break. "I wanted to see if I could do anything for him, too."

"I guess you didn't," Dr. Dinger said with a sigh. "Cheryl was still there with his parents when she went into hard labor."

"Yeah," I admitted. "I don't know why though."

"Nothing seems to be wrong with Reggie on a physical or biological level," Dr. Dinger said. "I checked his file myself, at his parents' request."

"What's wrong with this little one?" I asked, still upset that my power was nowhere to be found. Maybe if I knew the problem, I would be able to help better? I wondered.

"Cheryl had preeclampsia," Dr. Dinger explained. "She was already at risk because she wasn't supposed to get pregnant again. And she's not exactly … "

"Laid back?" I suggested, and he gave me a rueful smile as the baby settled against me and began to move.

"He likes you," Dr. Dinger said.

"But I haven't fixed him completely," I whispered, suddenly afraid I would fail, like I had before, with Reggie. "Maybe … "

My instinct to save and protect kicked into high gear. I was suddenly angry at myself. Why couldn't I seem to save anyone? I'd lost that man, Joe, and now I couldn't heal Reggie, and I couldn't heal this baby!

It seemed as though I was only able to save myself. I thought about how I was able to strengthen myself when the techs took my blood, and when my power unleashed and I was able to transform into my Starlight Warrior self …

I thought back to the papers from Dr. Dinger's office and suddenly had hope again. "Use my blood, then."

"He would benefit from a transfusion." He hesitated. "Are you sure?"

"You know it will work," I reminded him. "All I ask in return is your promise to keep silent about this. My grandpa would not be happy with me doing anything like this right now. It's lucky he is not here."

Dr. Dinger sighed. "I saw him on my way down," he said. "He said he would meet you at home, since I thought you were going to schedule another appointment."

"He is very protective of me," I said. "And I know he would be upset at me for this."

Dr. Dinger clasped my shoulder, before he finished hooking me up to the IV. "You have my word I will not breathe a word to anyone about this," he said. "We will never speak of it again, if you would like."

"I would."

I held the baby as he received my blood, and instantly, the world around me seemed to right itself. I was too tired to transform, but my blood held my own power in it, and I wanted to protect this baby.

As the blood dripped through the IV between us, I glanced over at Dr. Dinger.

"You can't tell anyone about this," I reiterated, "and that includes the Skarmastad Foundation."

He frowned. "But think of all the good you could do," he said. "There are millions of people who need this sort of treatment. You could help them, and the Skarmastad Foundation has the resources to help."

I shook my head. "I would be destroyed in the end," I said. "I'm happy to give blood when I can, as you know. But this

182

isn't something other people should know about. There are plenty of people who would use this sort of power for the wrong reasons." As I echoed Grandpa Odd's words, I felt a sense of dread. He'd warned me about using my power. I hoped it would not anger him.

Dr. Dinger sighed. "I suppose you're right," he said softly. "And I did promise you. I won't say anything."

Several moments went by, and I allowed myself to enjoy the tiny baby as he squirmed more restlessly in my arms. I wondered at the magic of holding that small life, and my heart ached, wishing I would be able to have my own children one day.

Dr. Dinger looked thoughtful, as the baby began to wriggle around more. "But I would love to know if there is a way to replicate the effect."

"You can try," I said. "But I doubt it would work."

"Why does your blood cure people?" Dr. Dinger asked.

"You don't know why?" I asked.

"I know what I see," he said, "and what I have read. But the underlying reasons, I don't know. Can you tell me?"

"No." I shook my head. "No, I can't."

"I figured as much," he replied with a rueful smile.

We said nothing else.

Even though I would now have to face the reality of keeping half-secrets from Dr. Dinger even more carefully, I knew I had done the right thing.

I still believed this several moments later when security came bursting into the room, followed by the midwife. Cheryl had apparently threatened a lawsuit to get them to do her bidding.

They slammed through the door, just to see me hand Dr. Dinger his son, who was not only alive, but thriving. Dr. Dinger smoothed things over with everyone, protecting me throughout the ordeal.

Soon after, I watched as Dr. Dinger handed the baby over to Cheryl, who was still reeling post-birth, I even felt her scorn was well worth it.

Cheryl was reluctant to give me credit, but I had a feeling that, after I left, she wouldn't bother me about what she'd seen in Reggie's room. I was okay with that trade off.

I left Dr. Dinger and Cheryl alone in her hospital room, letting them sit with their son, who was in perfect health.

That image stayed with me, until I finally realized how weak I was. I was stumbling around, looking for a place to rest, when I saw Grandpa at the entrance to the emergency room's waiting area.

"Raiya, why are you still here?" he asked, coming up beside me. "I went home, looking for you."

I ignored his questions. "I'm tired," I told him instead. "I want to go home."

And then I fainted.

☼13☼
The Point Where the Light and Shadow Meet

When I woke up again, things seemed to revert mostly back to normal.

Or at least, my new version of normal.

I woke up in my bed to another bright August day, and it really seemed like a lifetime since everything was ruined.

There was a knock at the door and I looked over just in time to see Rachel poke her head into my room.

"Hey, it's almost time for you to get up and go to school," she said.

"Thanks," I said. "How long have I been asleep?"

"Grandpa brought you home from the hospital yesterday," Rachel said. "You were barely able to walk. You went up to bed and that was it."

"Oh." My stomach suddenly growled, and Rachel laughed.

"I'm making breakfast," she said. "Come on down and I'll get you a chai, too."

I looked out my window again, glancing across the city streets to the sunlit hills and the lake in the distance. "I guess I've missed enough school," I agreed, and hurried to get ready.

"Raiya?"

"What is it?" I asked, glancing back at Rachel while I tried to find a new pair of clean socks in my drawer.

"Your friend Jeff is here. He wanted to walk you to school."

I must've looked confused or afraid, or some degree of both, because Rachel shook her head. "He's not interested in dating," she promised. "He mentioned that Chelsea and Ayah said something to him and he wanted to see if he could talk to you about it."

"Oh."

My movements became more jerky, more stagnant, but I still pushed through as much as I could. If I was going to get lectured about Chelsea and Ayah's grief with me, let alone by the one person I would let lecture me, I would have to face it.

I walked down to the living room, and Jeff greeted me with a wave as he finished talking to Rachel.

"That sounds great," Jeff said, and then Rachel saw me as well.

"What's great?" I asked, chiming in as though it had been my cue.

"Jeff's band is looking for a new venue," Rachel said. "So I said I would see if my boss would let them perform at the restaurant."

"Good luck." I sat down next to Jeff at the small kitchen table. Rachel handed me a plate full of eggs and weird-looking pancakes (wild berry flavored, with ground-up blueberries and raspberries) and half a banana. "I know your boss is picky about things like that."

"True enough," Rachel said, suddenly much less eager.

"I'd love to get them into a few places before I move," Jeff said.

"You're moving?" Rachel asked.

"Yeah. My dad wants to live without winter," Jeff told her, and I only half-listened as they chatted some more. I was waiting for Jeff to bring up our friends' complaints, and as much as I knew I would likely give better results and make nicer promises to apologize in front of Rachel, Jeff didn't subject me to that.

After Rachel started getting ready to go to her own class at the college, we headed out toward Rosemont Academy.

"She's very nice," Jeff said.

I nodded. "Rachel's more like a sister to me than a cousin," I agreed. "I hope her boss will let you play."

"Me, too," Jeff said. "And I'd love for you to come, if we do."

I smiled, but I couldn't help but thinking how much I almost wished his gig would fall through, if that was the case.

"Rachel really likes music," Jeff continued. "She said that if she ever gets her own place, she wants to hold music nights."

THE STARLIGHT CHRONICLES

C. S. JOHNSON

"Sounds like a good crowd pleaser," I said. "You know, from a marketing and advertising perspective."

Jeff agreed, and we lapsed into silence for a few moments, before the inevitable sigh came. "Well, I guess Rachel already mentioned I wanted to talk about Ayah and Chelsea," he said.

I nodded. "I was hoping we could forget about it."

"Ayah's upset," he said. "And Chelsea's confused and hurt. I thought I would come by and see if there was some way I could help."

"No," I said, shaking my head. "I hurt Reggie, Jeff. Ayah won't forgive me for that. And there's nothing I can do to help him, either."

"Well, no one would expect you to do that," Jeff said. "That's why there are doctors, you know."

"I know." I knew, but I didn't believe. I thought about my blood again, how it had helped that little baby. Was that something that Reggie would need?

If he did, I vowed I would give it to him. I owed him that much, at the very least, for all his friendship. And I should try to heal him, given that I had broken his heart in the first place.

"What about Chelsea?" Jeff asked. "Have you tried talking to her about it?"

"No," I admitted. "I don't want to bother with it anymore, Jeff."

THE STARLIGHT CHRONICLES

He frowned. "It seems like such a small thing to lose your friendship over," he pointed out.

I was tempted to tell him that there were bigger reasons why losing our friendship wouldn't bother me when I saw it again.

My wrist was sprinkled with pain. The Emblem of the Prince was calling.

There is a monster nearby, I realized. *And Jeff is in danger.*

"You know what?" I turned to Jeff. "I'm tired of this drama. I don't want to be friends with them anymore. Ayah thinks I hurt Reggie, and maybe I did, but I'm not going to be friends with people who think I'd do that to my friends."

"But they're upset and confused," Jeff argued.

"Well, let them be upset and confused on their own," I said. "I don't want to have anything to do with them anymore."

Go away. Go away, please. I need to transform, and I need to save you.

"I can understand Ayah getting on your nerves," Jeff continued.

At that moment, I could have sworn he was doing it to annoy me more than anything.

"Just stop, Jeff," I said. "Please, just go on to school without me. I forgot something at my house. I don't want to talk about this anymore, okay? And please let Ayah and Chelsea know I'd really like just not to hang out anymore."

Jeff scowled at me. "Come on, that's not fair," he said.

"So what?" I asked. "Life is not fair, and I know that more than anyone!"

The darkness was creeping up on me again, and I was getting more desperate to let him go.

"But you can't just stop being our friend," Jeff insisted.

"Sure I can," I said, throwing my hands up. "Reggie decided that I could stop being his friend in order to be his girlfriend. Why I can't I do the opposite?"

Jeff shrunk back from me, finally. I let out a small sigh of relief.

"I know that change happens," Jeff said. "And *I* know that better than anyone, don't I? But I never thought you would be like this, Raiya."

My cheeks started to fluster. "Well, it's no concern of yours, is it?" I asked, hating myself for being so mean. "You'll be gone in a few weeks, and it'll be like you were never here to begin with."

At that, Jeff shook his head. "I'm out of here," he said. "I guess I'll see you around school, but don't feel the need to talk to me."

For a moment, his words filled me with enough sadness to make me sick. But as the demon shadow drew closer to me, I knew I could only dig in my heels. "I won't!" I called after him.

I didn't know if he heard me. He had his back to me, and he never looked back.

Pain trickled into my wrist once more, and I grimaced. I hurried into a nearby alley and pressed down on my mark.

Instantly, I felt a tidal wave of power overcome me. It was only after I saw everything—my gloves, my tunic, my boots, and my wings—that I let myself realize I should be relieved.

My power was working normally.

My new idea of "normally," at least.

Despite my immense gratitude, I had no time to appreciate it. I saw the demon shadow move quickly around the corner.

Following after it, I took to the skies. My wings beat hard and fast, while the sunlight was warm on my body and the wind whipped all around me.

"Yashool," the demon whispered, and I caught sight of it.

It looked at me through hollow eyes, and I was reminded once more of Almeisan, my beloved Star. Before I could ask him, he swirled away, heading out toward Rosemont.

"Come back," I called, angry and frustrated that I couldn't reach him.

I called forth my power, balling it into my fists. The energy crackled angrily, seeming to reflect my own feelings on the matter.

After taking careful aim, I launched it.

The energy crackled out from me like a bolt of lightning; I felt the strength of it, as it blew back against me. I faltered in my flying, watching in awe and horror as the demon slipped around the small cord of power.

My energy hit my school, on the second floor. It broke through the brick, and I cringed as part of the wall began to crumble dangerously.

If there was ever a reminder for me that Grandpa was right, that I should never reveal the truth of who or what I was to anyone, it was that. I squirmed at the thought of Rachel worrying about us paying for city damages. The Skarmastad Foundation could only take care of so many of my medical bills. I was very grateful that Rachel was on her last semester of college, or I worried she would give that up, too.

"Yashool!"

The demon's cry brought me back to where I was and the immediate concerns I had on my hands.

My wings fluttered quickly, and I hurried over to where he was headed.

"Almeisan," I cried, hoping he would hear me and I could somehow find a way to cure him once more.

193

The demon didn't stop; he kept flying around, like a ghostly wraith.

Some of the people on the streets saw him and began to scream. I hopped down onto the city streets, unwilling to have my own picture in the newspaper.

They would probably think I was the villain anyway, I thought with a groan, remembering the other article I'd read before.

I chased him through the city alleyways; I leaped over fences, ducked under signs, slipped through cracks, and jumped over broken ledges.

When I found myself behind the hospital, I stopped. I was panting hard, but my power remained steadfast. Though I had been stymied in my mission, I was still ready to fight.

But the demon monster was no longer in sight. I looked down at my wrist, hoping the Emblem of the Prince would give me a clue.

There was nothing.

Nothing.

I wanted to scream in frustration.

But instead, I took a deep breath. I pressed the mark, and allowed myself to fade into my regular self.

I will get him one day, I silently vowed.

As I turned around and headed back toward the street, I had to wonder if he was really Almeisan's ghostly remnant. He hadn't reacted at all when I called him.

The memory shuffled between my thoughts again. The demon had the same eyes as I'd seen on Almeisan, before he'd been transformed and given his new name. But that didn't mean that it was the same demon, right?

I thought about the face I'd been painting, only half-conscious of what I was doing that day that I rammed my fist into the wall where my mural was not even halfway finished.

His eyes were blue, like the sea lit up with sunshine.

I shook my head, placing my hand over my heart. Almeisan was gone, I told myself. I'd lost him. I destroyed him. He was gone. We were both gone.

"Raiya?"

I turned, surprised to see Dr. Dinger. "Hello, Dr. Dinger."

"What are you doing here?" he asked. He suddenly looked hopeful. "Did you change your mind about the blood?"

"Blood?" I felt myself torn away from my other world once more. I sank back into the present moment, where I had to deal with my actions.

All of my actions, I thought wryly.

"No," I finally said.

195

"Oh." Dr. Dinger looked a little deflated. "I guess you're here to see your friend again, then?"

I suddenly recalled my original purpose in going to see Dr. Dinger, when his son was born. I had wanted him to allow me to see Reggie, and I had been sidetracked by saving his baby and then by my exhaustion. I didn't want Dr. Dinger to let anyone use my blood for experiments; that would only lead to a witch hunt, like Grandpa had told me. But maybe … maybe I could do it myself, alone, so Dr. Dinger would not know what I was doing?

I just needed Dr. Dinger to let me into his room.

That was what I wanted, I decided.

"Yes," I said. "I'm here to see Reggie."

"Skipping school's never a good idea," he said pointedly.

I nodded. "I know," I said. "But … but I'm worried for him. I don't think I'd be able to do a lot of good at school anyway."

Dr. Dinger seemed to understand. "His parents aren't here," he said, and I knew he was trying to tell me that I would have to sneak in if I wanted to see him. "But I'll see you at your next appointment, alright?"

"Sounds good. Thank you." I gave him a bright smile, and I think he knew that I was telling him I was grateful for the information as well as the opportunity he was allowing me to have.

It seemed he was going to keep our promise, after all. I said a silent prayer of thanks for that. In revealing my secret power to him, I had unknowingly thrown us into a web of secrets. It was unnerving that our secrets could build walls between us as well as bring us closer together.

But then, I looked into my own soul, and I knew that the weirdest paradoxes of life were often where truth resided. The demon monster had darkened my day, but my power was full of light. It had brought me to this place, where I would test my power once more.

Reggie's coma was a dark stain on my mission, but I was determined to turn it into a victory.

As I headed up the stairs to his room, I walked into the shadows; I felt more certain than ever that there was something both good and great that gave me power, and that I was going to save Reggie no matter what.

☼14☼
The Unraveling of Time

My steps were silent as I made my way toward Reggie's side.

Dr. Dinger had been right; neither of Reggie's parents were in sight, and I was glad for this. Tomas would only make me think of that day I'd transformed and tried to save people in the collapsing underground ... what was it anyway, a lab?

As for Kaya, she would remind me of a mother's desperate love, and it didn't take much for that thought to hop over to Cheryl, and for that to transform into fears about legal matters.

Legal matters which, I knew, included the laws I was likely breaking.

I glanced down at Reggie again. He had not changed much since yesterday, I thought to myself, if he had changed at all. He still seemed frozen in time. Even his hair seemed to share that quality. Each dreadlock lay against his freshly-fluffed pillows, unmoving.

I glanced over at the IV, and I wondered if I could find a way to get my blood into that. It was the simplest way, honestly, since I didn't have a medical degree or any training.

But I did have years of giving blood, I reminded myself. I thought of all the ways that I had been pricked and plugged by the nurse techs and doctors.

I found a small pair of medical scissors and used it to cut a sliver in my wrist, right through the Emblem of the Prince. I nearly gasped in pain, and I had to remind myself not to heal myself right away.

As my blood dripped onto the floor, I grabbed the IV bag. Upon close examination, I found a small port near the top of the bag, but I would need a needle to inject my blood into it. I ignored it a moment later, going for the tubing port instead. I pulled the tubing out of the bag, and placed it next to my blood. Several drops went inside, and I cheered.

I let several moments go by before I decided that was enough. I was feeling weak again, and I didn't know if it would work anyway.

After all, I thought, the baby had needed a transfusion, according to what Dr. Dinger told me. Nothing was physically wrong with Reggie.

My healing power flooded over my wrist, and the blood stopped.

And that's when another revelation hit me.

My power was able to heal anything about myself, I realized. *Except* …

Except my broken heart.

How many times had I come to the hospital for that very reason?

I had plenty of power, but my heart was broken.

I looked over at Reggie again. My blood was likely flooding into his system, but there was no change.

I'd broken Reggie's heart.

I wanted to heal him on instinct—just the way I wanted to heal Jeff of his broken heart, and I had been unable to.

My thoughts went back to that moment again, that moment when I'd grabbed at Reggie, trying to get his heart to stop breaking.

I looked down at my hands. My power had called out, like it never had before.

Never on this side of Time, anyway, I thought. I was desperate to save my friend from a broken heart, and because of that … I would willingly condemn him to something worse.

"Reggie," I gasped, as I figured it out. I reached for my power again. My hand lit up with my violet power, and I pushed further in, to take me back to that moment.

I saw his Soulfire as I watched, and I nearly cheered to see I was right.

His Soulfire was the same as it had been the second before I'd attacked him. It was a collapsing star, all the bright kindness falling into itself.

But as I held my power constant, I saw the difference. There was a silvery fog wrapped around his soul, and it wasn't supposed to be there.

I reached out with my hand carefully.

The wispy light inside of Reggie blurred as I got closer. My fingers drifted over it, and it felt like silk.

And when I finally took hold of it, it slipped into my hand as though it had been waiting for me to find it. I felt it slide onto my bloodied arm and sink into the liquid power. The small patch winked up at me from my wrist in the dim light, and I suddenly couldn't look away from it.

Then, Reggie gasped, and began to thrash around in his bed.

"Reggie," I whispered, relieved and amazed.

My mouth dropped open in surprise, even as Reggie began to wake up. His heart monitor began to beep more quickly.

But all of this faded into the background, as I allowed myself to fall back into my own mind.

"I know what this is," I heard myself whisper. "This is part of Time's barrier."

What was it doing inside of me?

I didn't know, but even just looking at it, I knew it was an object of great power.

The fabric of Time's power.

It didn't take me any time to know I would have to hide this. I remembered what Grandpa had told me. If I wasn't able to save myself from temptation, no one would be safe. Everything would be lost.

And, I decided, as I looked down at Reggie waking up, I was tired of things being lost. The little speckles of blood from my arm tempered some of the light, and I knew I could hide it, until I figured out what to do with it.

I thought about asking Grandpa, but when Reggie's eyes opened up, I quickly hid the fabric, and my blood-covered arm, behind my back.

"Raiya." Reggie's hand reached out, grabbing onto my free hand. I stiffened, but I allowed myself a moment. Of all of my friends, I owed Reggie the most—and perhaps, I thought, that meant that I owed him a proper goodbye.

"Reggie," I said. "Thank goodness you're awake."

"Where am I?" he asked, his eyes going wide as he looked around. "What happened?"

"I'm … I'm not sure," I said, even though I finally knew what had happened for certain.

I'd tried to stop his heart from breaking, and at my own inability to do this, I'd wrapped his heart up in Time's power, and stopped it from breaking completely.

I gripped the shimmering airiness of Time's fabric in my hand behind my back. What a small, seemingly weak thing it was, and yet it had caused so much trouble. On some level, I was relieved. On other levels, I had a new piece of the puzzle that told me who I was, and I had to deal with that.

And that meant I would have to deal with that without Reggie and my other friends.

"How long have I been in here?" Reggie asked. He tugged at my hand, seeming to forget that he'd reached for it only a moment before.

We both looked down at his darkened hands, as they intertwined with my knuckles. For a long moment, neither of us said anything.

And then I sighed and pulled away. "You've been in here for about two and a half weeks," I said. Reggie sighed, and I didn't have to guess why.

"That long, huh?" Reggie shifted his weight, trying to scoot up against his pillows.

"Yeah."

"I guess I have a lot of school work waiting for me," he said, giving me one of his kind smiles. I saw his Soulfire spark up before me, at only half-light.

"You and me both," I assured him. "I've missed a lot of school while you were out, too."

"Need a homework buddy?" he asked, and that spark seemed to brighten.

"No thanks," I said. I decided to shift the focus. "You know, I'm sure Ayah would love to help you. She's been very worried about you since you came here."

"I guess I can't blame her, if I can't even remember why I'm in here."

"Well, I'm sure your doctor or your parents will be able to help with that," I said.

It went quiet between us, and that was the moment I hesitated.

How could I tell him that we couldn't be friends anymore?

Suddenly, he laughed. "I guess I know my answer, then," he said.

I felt my knees go weak. "What are you talking about?" I asked, my voice barely a whisper.

"I'm remembering it now," he said. "You didn't want to go out on a date with me, did you?"

Numbness tingled through me, and I barely realized I nodded.

He sighed. "I had a feeling that would be my answer."

"I'm sorry," I whispered. "You've always been a good friend. I just ... I just don't feel that way about you. I'm not meant ... I mean, I'm not really looking to date anyone."

Reggie gave me one of his kind smiles. "You didn't have to attack me over it," he said. "You could have just told me no."

"I didn't attack you," I said, my voice flat. Suddenly, it was a lot easier to make excuses.

"I remember you coming at me," Reggie said. "And then everything went really still. I feel like I've been pulled out of a void."

At that, I was *really* ready to go.

"Well, I'll see you around school," I said, backing up. "I've got a lot of work to catch up on myself, and your parents will be very happy to see you."

"Raiya," Reggie said. "It's alright. Everything's alright. You don't have to leave."

"Yes, I do," I said quietly. "I'm glad you're awake. See you later."

"Raiya! Come on! Come back," Reggie called.

But it was too late. I'd made my decision, and I hurried out of the room, ducking out just in time to avoid being seen by a nurse.

As I tucked myself behind the stairway door, I saw the nurse reappear, with a smile on her face. She was probably going to tell the hospital to notify Reggie's parents.

I was really happy he was okay, even if it meant seceding all my rights to his friendship at last.

I gripped the fabric of Time in my hand. It shimmered again. "Let's go home," I said, talking to it. I did have to wonder if Lady Time was able to hear me through it.

As it shimmered once more, I realized that even if she could, Lady Time likely didn't think I was being anywhere close to appropriate or amusing. The fabric itself was far from its home.

I sighed. Neither of us were anywhere close to being home, I thought.

☼15☼

Time, Space, and Space-Time between Friends

I felt more than a little disoriented after I left the hospital. It was a school day, and one which I was taking an unauthorized leave of; I had managed to save Reggie from a coma, even if I couldn't save him from disappointment; and I had found a piece of Time's power, which had been lingering around inside of me.

There were a couple of things I could do, I thought. I could hide the fabric and hope that I would learn enough about the Immortal Realm to return it to Lady Time one day.

If I didn't forget about it in the meantime.

I supposed I could also tell Grandpa about it. But it would involve risking Reggie's involvement, and I didn't want to drag him into it.

What if Grandpa told me to double-check Reggie's heart for more of the fabric? I mean, it didn't seem like the kind of material that would break easily, but I could see Grandpa insisting I check. It was a powerful thing, and it only seemed to be tempered by my blood.

I didn't want to do that. I didn't want to bother Reggie's life any more than I already had.

I could also try to destroy it, but I had a feeling that would do nothing to help me in Adonaias' eyes, either.

My face fell as I thought about that. I had used my Star's wish to recapture my sisters. My power had broken through the fabric of Time.

"Maybe that's why I'm here," I said, muttering to myself.

The scene played out logically enough in my mind. My sisters broke free from me, likely with someone's help or through trickery; I used my Star's wish to recapture them, and in using my power, my Star went supernova, blasting a hole through Lady Time's power, and somehow, that sent me flying into the Moral Realm, clothed with human flesh despite my supernatural soul.

I frowned. That didn't sound *wrong*, but it didn't sound right, either.

My mental debate raged on as I walked through the streets to my home.

Rachel was already gone for the day. Aunt Letty was sitting at the kitchen table as I entered.

She groaned. "Not again, Raiya. Please, do I have to write another excuse for you?"

I arched my brow at her. "Do I have to tell Rachel that you're smoking in the house again?" I asked, nodding to the cigarette in her hand.

She rubbed the lit end of it into the humming ashtray in front of her. "Fine," she said. "We've reached an agreement."

I might have laughed, if she didn't see my blood-covered arm.

THE STARLIGHT CHRONICLES

"What happened there?" Aunt Letty asked. "Get into a fight?"

"Sort of," I muttered. "I didn't get to school."

"Was it that boy who came here earlier?" Aunt Letty reached over and tossed me a towel. "Was he the one you fought?"

"Jeff?" I shook my head. "No, it wasn't him."

"Well, tell me what you want written in your letter of absence," Aunt Letty said. "You'd better tell me quick, too, because they've been calling more."

"Calling?"

"Yes, to know where you're at."

"That's weird."

"After ten days, it's what they do," Aunt Letty said. She stood and cleaned up her incriminating evidence, before she sighed. "It's only the third week of school, Raiya. If you're gone so many days, they'll drop your registration. It's not good."

She didn't have to tell me that.

"Maybe I could get Dr. Dinger to write a note," I said, thinking of how much I did go and see him. It seemed like it would be enough to appease my schoolroom overlords, anyway, I thought with a wry smile.

"It's not a bad idea. In fact, that would be best," Aunt Letty said. "So, what should I tell the school this time?"

"Tell them I had a medical relapse," I said. "It's close enough."

It wasn't a lie. My heart was broken, and I'd just broken it again several times, between telling Jeff off and telling Reggie I didn't want to be around him.

Aunt Letty snorted. "Fine by me," she said. "I had worse excuses in my day. Of course, they didn't care if you came or not, let alone graduated. Now they have all those quotas on student rates."

"That's true," I said with a quick laugh. "You and I fight the system, either way, I guess."

She gave me one of her rare, whole-face smiles. "Well, that might be the case, but this fighter is going back to bed. I had a long night, and it was a longer night than it had to be with that guy I went out with."

"New one?" I asked.

She stuck out her tongue distastefully. "Yes," she said. "But he's old news now. I got another date tonight with his best friend."

I said nothing as Aunt Letty went up to her room. I could hear her shaking her bottle of sleeping pills as I walked into my room.

Personally, I was just glad that, even though she'd seen my arm, she paid no attention to what I was holding in my other hand.

I pulled out the fabric again, studying it. It was made of light, little ribbons of pure energy running through in a pattern too simple and too delicate for me to pull apart.

It was time to find a good hiding place for it. Somewhere I would always remember it, but no one else would suspect it.

Eventually, I pulled down a blank canvas from my small collection.

I quickly decided to paint something—not one of my usual works, but something that would make me think of the fabric of Time. Something that reminded me of Reggie, and my other friends, and how important it was to protect them, and how important it was to distance myself from them.

A smile crept onto my face as I made my decision. "I have the perfect idea," I said, and hurriedly got to work.

Hours later, I heard a knock at my door. I swirled around, knowing there was no way to get the paint off my face without getting more on it. "Who is it?" I asked.

"It's me," Grandpa called, and I immediately felt guilty.

THE STARLIGHT CHRONICLES

"Give me a moment," I said, hurrying to make sure that my paint, especially the cups which contained my mix of blood, were closed up.

It was only after I was relatively cleaned up that I opened my door. "What is it, Grandpa?" I asked.

"I just talked with Letty about your absence from school today," he said. There was a disapproving look beneath his beard and mustache.

I sighed. "I saw a demon today," I admitted. "He looked like a *bakreel,* and I followed him, trying to find a way to destroy him, I guess."

Grandpa sighed. "I was worried about this."

"Next time, I'll make sure I get to school right after," I promised. "I just … got sidetracked."

It was his turn to arch his brow at me, and I almost relented. But at the last second, I thought of Reggie and I knew I had to honor my promise to protect him.

"You should have come and got me," Grandpa said.

"I didn't know where you were," I admitted, and that was the truth. "I came home and just tried to … calm down, and paint some."

I glanced back at my picture, where I knew the fabric of Time was hidden under several layers of blood and paint.

Grandpa frowned. "That's not your usual style," he said.

THE STARLIGHT CHRONICLES

"Well," I said, "I thought maybe I would try something different. You know I have people in art class that complain my work is too dreamy, and all that."

"What is it, then?" Grandpa asked.

"It's a neo-expressionist supernova," I said quietly, hoping he would not ask any more questions.

I looked at it as he did, trying to see it through Reggie's eyes. He was the one who was all about neo-expressionism anyway.

The supernova was a good reminder to me, too, about the danger of failing, about the danger of getting close to people, about the danger of risking eternal promises for temporal joys.

It would remind me for years that there was a price too great for me to pay to slip up again.

"I like it," Grandpa finally said. "It's different, as I said, from your usual style, but it's very good. Something very powerful about the center of the explosion, too."

"Well, it should be," I said. "That's where the fight goes on. Right, Grandpa? The battle between good and evil is always only one choice away."

He nodded. "I can see I've taught you well," he said. And then he gave me a quick pat on my head. It was something he had done before when I was a smaller child, and I reveled in that moment, collectively reliving his approval.

And then the moment passed.

213

"But," Grandpa added, "you might love your painting too much."

"What do you mean?" I asked, hoping once more he would not ask about the painting.

"There's a demon on the move," he said. "I've felt it getting stronger throughout the day. I think you should go and check it out."

"Oh." I looked down at my wrist, and I frowned. "I wonder why I didn't feel it myself?"

Grandpa nodded toward my easel again. "It really is a lovely painting," he said. "Maybe you were just too distracted."

I laughed nervously. "I guess so," I said. It was at that moment that I felt the first tremor of demonic power twinge through me.

"I feel it now," I said. "I'll go and see what's happening."

"Good." Grandpa nodded. "Please, Raiya. Be careful. You know how I feel about you. I would be remiss if anything happened to you."

"You know what's going to happen before it does, more often than not," I reminded him. "You know that I'll be okay."

He shrugged. "The future is already clear, but not always," he said. "It's both being made and already made, and I can only read between the lines."

214

It was sometimes hard to understand my grandfather. I knew that he lived out of Time as much as he lived in Time, and that paradox was more noticeable to a fallen Star like me. But I had the distinct impression that humans—full human beings, I mean—felt that way too. Like there was more to this life, and it was real, but it was unable to be proven.

I locked my bedroom door as I headed out.

"Be careful," Grandpa reiterated. "I feel something strange happening."

I nodded. "I will." And then I headed out.

While I was out on a demon hunt, by myself, for the first official time with Grandpa's approval, despite all his worrying besides, I had to admit, I really loved flying.

The sky was dark enough that I did not feel the need to worry as much as I had earlier, when I was chasing Yashool around.

The air whipped at me, but in the few times I'd flown, I'd already gotten used to it. The brisk embrace now felt like a welcome back greeting, and the moonlight peeking through the last of the day's sunlight seemed like a timid hello from another world.

As I headed down into the city, I quickly forgot the magic of the night. My wrist bubbled with a new alert, warning me that there were monsters of all kinds just waiting to be called out.

I felt a surge of pain inside of me as I headed toward Rosemont Academy. In the evening light, I could see the hole I'd nearly blasted through the one school wing was still there, with police and construction tape blocking off the area below.

I landed on the campus green, the small, grassy area outside of the school's main entrance. Looking around, I saw nothing, but I felt several streams of power calling out to me.

"Where are you?" I asked, hoping that the monster could hear me, for one, and didn't think I sounded like a wimp, for another.

I felt the hollow energy circling around me, and I turned to see that there were three shadows coming my way.

"Yashool," came the whispered cry, and I felt the back of my legs tingle in alarm.

"No," I gasped, as I realized that the demons had captured my friends.

My eyes became wet with tears as I saw Jeff, Chelsea, and Ayah. They were all were unconscious, as a trio of ghostly spirits grappled with them.

I was trapped, surrounded with them and their power.

"This is impossible," I whispered. "How——?"

Ayah's mouth moved, even though her eyes were closed. "Surely you shouldn't be so surprised, Lady Justice?"

The voice coming out of her body was not hers.

"Who are you?" I demanded to know.

"What does it matter?" the voice asked through Chelsea this time. "We know who you are, and why you've come."

"Then you know your battle is with me, not these kids," I said. I clenched my fists angrily, allowing my power to feed into my palms.

The demon laughed, his voice echoing through all three of them.

"I've been watching you carefully," he said. "Your power is great, and difficult to hide."

I thought of the fabric of Time, as it was hiding in my room at my house. Was it putting Rachel and Grandpa and Aunt Letty in danger, too?

Renewed frustration hit me all over. Why did this demon seem so determined to pick on me personally? It wasn't enough that it had to try to destroy me or capture my power, he had to do it through my friends, too.

I held up my fists, preparing to fight as Grandpa taught me. "If you came here for my power, you're going to have to fight me for it."

"I figured that was what you would say," the demon said, talking through Jeff this time. I whirled around, trying to keep pace with his movements, as he swapped out my friends. "So I came prepared this time."

"Prepared?"

"Yes," the demon hissed delightfully. "Your friends make the perfect shield."

I forced myself not to allow him to affect me. "They aren't my friends," I told him.

"Well, they were certainly upset over you before," the demon said.

My eyes were rapidly filling with tears, as the demon continued to taunt me.

"This one," he said, nodding to Chelsea, "wondered what she'd done to you, that made you turn away from her after all these years."

"She didn't do anything!" I yelled back. "Chelsea," I called, turning my focus to her. "You didn't do anything. You're smart and talented and you'll make a great computer engineer one day!"

Nothing happened.

"And this one," the demon murmured playfully, as he thrust Jeff onto the ground in front of me, "hated to think that he made the rift between you and the others worse."

"No, he didn't," I insisted, but I began to realize I was arguing in a battle that was very familiar.

THE STARLIGHT CHRONICLES

I jumped up and took flight, hurriedly dodging out of the circle of my possessed friends.

"Yashool," the demon monster howled. "I see your power has grown much in the last few days. Perhaps the dragon's power is weakening as well, if he can't control you."

"Dragon? Control me?" I shook my head as I landed behind Ayah. "No one controls me. Not even the Prince stopped me when I ripped through Time."

The demon laughed, and I took the second he was distracted to lash out an attack.

My power shot out of me hard and fast. I barely had the chance to aim it. It was louder than I remembered, too, and the wings beside my ears tingled with the soundwaves. For the spilt second where my light shone brightly against his cloudy body, I squeezed my eyes shut.

I heard the demon growl, and I began to move again. The years of fighting techniques Grandpa had taught me took over, and I was grateful for that.

Scooting to the side, I looked over to see that I'd nearly hit Chelsea. "Gotta aim better," I muttered to myself, but I was pleased to see that I'd managed to cut through some of his power. Jeff's body, limp and helpless before, was now face down on the ground and still.

Quickly, I took careful aim, and sent out another blast. I cried out in frustration as the demon, with only two captives now, seemed to be faster.

I prepared to use another shot of power, but Yashool only laughed.

Glaring at him, I held back. "What's so funny?" I yelled.

"You, of course," he said. "It's always such fun toying with a novice."

"Novice or not, I'm still going to beat you," I said.

"Not with that lack of finesse," Yashool taunted. "And you'll never fully defeat me on your own."

"Why's that?" I asked, grunting as he slipped around me, lashing out an attack of his own. His claws clipped my tunic, but the strong armor kept his power at bay.

My friends flopped around next to me, as we all fell to the ground. I put a hand in front of them, trying to use my power to cut through their bonds. Chelsea fell free, joining Jeff on the ground, but Ayah remained tangled in the demon's web of power.

"You mean you haven't figured it out yet?" Yashool laughed at me again. "You'll need to do better than that," he taunted, before he tugged Ayah up next to his face. "Well, this has been lovely, but we'll have to see you later."

He jumped into the air, pulling Ayah after him.

"Wait!" I called.

At my cry, Yashool turned around. "You know, I really should thank you," he said. "Not only were the other two more of a drain on my power, but you've only added to my power with your despair."

I jumped, ready to take flight after him.

But then, Yashool unleashed a storm of power of his own. The wave slammed into me, driving me back into the ground. It kept coming, and I hurried to shield Jeff and Chelsea from the attack.

When the flow of power stopped, I was left looking up at a clear night sky.

Yashool was gone, and Ayah was gone, too.

"No!" I shouted, too anguished to say anything else. I fell against the grassy lawn, thrusting my fists into the ground hard, unable or unwilling to recover from my loss.

☼16☼
Failure Comes Just Before Hitting Rock Bottom

It was about an hour later that I felt my inner resolve start to reform.

Of course, I had been diligent about getting my friends taken care of, even though I had gone through the steps as though I was sleeping, as if my brain was on autopilot.

I barely heard the ambulance as it arrived, even though I was the one who called it in. I tended to Jeff and Chelsea's wounds as much as I could, but after my battle, I already felt drained of my power and my resolve. I had shifted back into my regular self, letting the cool grass nip at me through my Rosemont uniform.

Why did he go after my friends? How did he know about them anyway?

I was too upset to contemplate the ramifications of these questions.

All I could think about was how I'd lost my friends. I'd cut off my friends in hoping it would save them, only to find they were in danger regardless. And as I sat there, helpless on the ground, I didn't know how I was going to fix it.

"Grandpa was right," I muttered, dropping my head into my hands. "I'm not ready for this."

The Emblem of the Prince on my wrist flickered, as if to tell me that wasn't the case. But in my grief, I felt like I imagined it. Maybe I did.

Jeff and Chelsea remained asleep on the ground, and I suddenly wondered if more was wrong than I'd originally thought.

My eyes darted to their hearts, and I saw that their Soulfire had been taken as well.

"No!" I stood up, dismayed and angry.

"Miss?" An emergency tech, one of the men from the ambulance, came up to me. "Are you alright?"

"*Nothing* is alright!" I snapped, before I turned away.

"Where are you hurt?" the man continued, a little less patiently.

"I'm not hurt," I said. "I ... I found these kids here." I waved over toward Jeff and Chelsea. "They need help."

They need help from someone who knows what they're doing, I thought bitterly. The cost of my power was too great if my friends were not going to survive, and I knew there was nothing that was going to wake them up without their Soulfire.

How long could they go without it? I wondered, and I had no answer to that. Grandpa might have said it was different, depending on the person, but even he couldn't be sure of that, could he?

The EMTs quickly got to work, picking up Jeff and Chelsea. Another one of them, a woman this time, came up to me and offered me a blanket.

223

I shook my head. I didn't deserve any comfort. I'd failed.

"Thank you for calling this in," the lady said. "Would you like to ride to the hospital with your friends?"

I shook my head again, before lowering my eyes to the ground. "They're not my friends," I whispered, and the EMT shrugged and headed off.

It must have been an hour that I watched over Jeff and Chelsea, before they disappeared.

I thought about going to the hospital. Really, I was sorely tempted to go.

But in the end, I just stood staring out at the grassy front lawn of Rosemont Academy, and I found myself unable to fathom how anything I could do would bring about anything good ever again.

"Adonaias," I whispered. "Where were you? Where *are* you?"

I retreated into myself once more, finding the memory of that night in Norway. I found myself looking for him in a cloud of dark water, looking for any sign that I would be able to overcome this.

"I know I have to fix so much," I said, muttering to myself. "I know I've caused so much pain and destruction, that I made terribly foolish choices and awful mistakes."

I fell into that memory.

"Let there be light," I murmured, trying to hear the soft strength of that voice again, and I nearly wept when nothing happened.

Nothing happened.

Why would something happen? I thought bitterly to myself. I'd failed, after all.

I've failed ... again.

My Star's wish, my beloved Almeisan, not saving Joe, not listening to Grandpa, accidentally using the fabric of Time to ground Reggie's heart into a moment of time forever ... all of those things, and the other failures and regrets came rushing over me, bathing me in shame and guilt.

"I've failed you so many times," I whispered. "I'm so sorry." The tears scattered down my cheeks, and I wanted to die, then and there.

If the pain hadn't been so real and paralyzing, I might have laughed. I'd dived into my meditation practice to find meaning, to find motivation, and to find a way to move forward. Yet, I found none of those things. All I found were the harsh truths of my reality.

I could have no friends. I could find no peace. I still had a lot of work to do, but no strength or courage to do it. I felt the full weight of justice on me, and I found myself condemned, with no hope to ever pay for my transgressions and shortcomings.

There was nothing just about me trying to earn my way back into the Celestial Kingdom's good graces, either. In many ways, I was dishonoring my love for Adonaias by believing that I could make up all my mistakes by working for him.

Especially, I thought with a grimace, after my rather poor performance earlier.

"Let there be light."

I blinked open my eyes. The memory in my mind had come alive before me, and I could see the Light again. Immediately, I nearly fell back at the brightness. Hurriedly, I moved to shield my eyes, but as my hand hurried up to my face, I felt something solid and heavy fall into it.

My curiosity made me forget the painful brilliance before me, as I examined the object I found myself holding.

It was a harp, strangely designed to fit my hands. It hovered off the ground as I reached out and strummed it, unable to resist.

Music poured from it—music from my past, and music from my future.

There was an unending song within me, and it did more than hold my memories. It held my love and affection and story and truth, and it gave me strength.

As I gripped it more tightly, I saw the harp transform in to a bow.

226

"The Bow of Righteousness," I murmured, its name coming to me in a supernatural stirring of my soul. I did not have to wonder about the conditions of it.

I took it and fit both hands over it, holding it ready. An arrow of light appeared, one of my own power and somehow more than my own power.

Renewed hope flourished within me. I had found, in my moment of brokenness, a shard of power, an instrument of truth and light.

I bowed my head over my new weapon. "Thank you," I whispered. And then, when I looked up, I saw that I had transformed once more, into my supernatural Starlight Warrior self.

I had a calling, a destiny, and a duty. It was time to embrace it, costs and all. My hand tightened around my bow, and I was determined to try again.

Failure is only final if the last move you make is falling down—and even then, sometimes all is not lost.

In that moment, I stood up tall, keeping my shoulders straight. I had more work to do.

THE STARLIGHT CHRONICLES

As I flew through the Apollo City skyline, my dark violet tunic blending into the night, I ran my fingers down my new weapon.

The bow was carved from wood in an elegant fashion; I wondered briefly if it was made from cedar wood, given my limited familiarity with wood from my various art classes of the past. It was layered with otherworldly material, it seemed, or maybe that was just its protection. I held it firmly, and it was as though it was made for me.

Which, given the divine origin of it and all, it likely was.

I watched as my power met the bowstring, a new arrow popping up at once. It was a wonder to see that it would come in handy; I hoped that if I missed, too, the damage would be far less noticeable.

That is, I thought, *if I can even find him again.*

My wrist was picking up nothing. I flew around the city and wondered what kind of game it was really playing with me.

Even though I continued to look for him, I allowed myself to fall back into that moment when he first attacked me.

Yashool was obviously a *bakreel* or a *fenfleal* demon, something that had to use a host for energy, or something that could overshadow the human mind, heart, and will so much that it could control the soul. But that was not the most disturbing part.

He'd come after me, specifically. *And* he'd used my friends as targets. He seemed to know who I was, even when I wasn't transformed into my supernatural self.

Why didn't he go after my family? I suddenly wondered. After a moment, it was easy enough to dismiss that. Grandpa had placed his own shield of protection on our house.

I briefly, fervently hoped it would hold. I had enough grief over my friends. Even though Reggie was awake, and Jeff and Chelsea were off to the hospital, I was still faced with the possibility that anyone I loved could be endangered.

I'd seen Yashool before. I'd seen him in the orchestra room, when I was with Jeff; he'd been in the hospital wing with Chelsea and Ayah, after I'd argued with them outside of Reggie's room.

He had been following *me*.

He is using me *as a host.*

The truth struck me and left me momentarily breathless. I dropped down to a nearby rooftop, keeping to the shadows, as I turned the idea over in my head.

I still didn't know how, but it made sense; my power was growing, and Grandpa had warned me about it signaling to other demons, and since his power was no longer able to hold mine back, it made some sort of sense that a *fenfleal* or *bakreel* monster would try to latch onto me.

I frowned for another moment. Yashool had mentioned that there was a dragon who was trying to control me. What had he meant by that? I wondered.

It was possible that he was lying. But there was no need for him to lie to me, was there? He had been pretty upfront about the rest, given that he held my friends hostage.

I looked out over the city, allowing myself to be distracted by the dazzling array of lights. It was a beautiful night. If I hadn't been tasked with protecting the city, I would have been a regular kid. I might have been hanging out with my friends as we grew up, smoothing out our awkwardness as we talked and laughed and joked together. I might have been visiting with Ayah, watching Jeff compose songs out of our collective class notes, or ice-skating with Chelsea and Reggie, staying late since his cousin was a manager at the ice rink.

Instead, I was flying around, looking for the monster who had stolen the souls of two of my friends, and held another friend hostage.

It was as I gazed over the rooftops, allowing my eyes to trace over the towering spirals, the sparkling clouds of breath and human life, that I noticed it.

There was a dim aura around the Time Tower.

I gripped my bow. I didn't have any other clues. I had no other leads. It wouldn't hurt to check it out.

It did feel a little out of place. What did I have to do with the Time Tower, after all? If Yashool was going to use me as his host, and try to destroy me or take over my power using every little bit of leverage he could, why didn't he choose somewhere else?

Even if my house was protected by Grandpa's power, and he didn't want to loop around back to the school, there was still the hospital, or Shoreside Park, or even the marina, where Joe had died under my watch.

I could have gone down this tangent for miles, asking myself questions about Yashool and his comments about the dragon, and my power, and all the other things about my friends. And I would have, too, if Yashool hadn't come flying toward me at that moment.

"So, you found me," he murmured, his voice grating against the soft moonlight.

"Where's Ayah?" I demanded, wanting to waste no time. "I know you're using her to get to me."

"Good," he said. "I admitted it freely to you, so you should know it. You're a smart one, despite your years here on Earth."

I flustered. It was hard not to feel like he was right.

Especially since he was, technically.

"Who are you?" I asked. "Are you Almeisan's demon ghost?"

Yashool laughed, and I had a hard time determining if he reminded me of Almeisan or not.

Almeisan wouldn't do this to me, I thought. But I wasn't sure. Would he make me suffer, if he had the chance? I destroyed him, after all, even if I loved him.

"What did you do with Ayah?" I asked again. Grandpa's rules had stuck. I needed to focus. I pulled up my bow, an arrow of light blazing before me. I grabbed it out of the air and steadied it against the bowstring.

"She's just getting some air," Yashool hissed, before one of his wispy hands lashed out, pointing back toward the Time Tower.

I saw Ayah, still unconscious and trapped in Yashool's power, as she was propped on a ledge on the roof, near the Time Tower's clock face.

"Ayah!" I propelled myself forward, but Yashool quickly got in my way.

"She doesn't have much time," he said, his voice cruel. "But you can have her back if you defeat me."

I frowned. "Your defeat was always a given," I retorted, but as his eyes grew round and soft, letting me see the full hollowness behind them, I wondered all over again if he was the ghost of my beloved.

My arrow lashed out at close range, knocking Yashool down from the sky.

He fell to the roof of a nearby building, and I hurried off after him.

THE STARLIGHT CHRONICLES

My bow was strong, and I used it to slice into his phantasmal body. I didn't defeat him, despite the power behind my blow. His body reformed, and he took to the air once more.

How do I defeat him? I desperately began to look for a weakness.

At that moment, as if to answer me, I saw a small bundle of light inside of the heart of his power.

I have to cut through his heart.

"I've got you now," I yelled, and I hurried to meet him with my power.

A large bubble of my power lit up in my palms, and I grabbed a hold of one of his airy limbs. I felt the light sink through him, scorching through his hollow darkness.

Yashool screamed, but then he latched his arm onto my wrist.

He held his power over the Emblem of the Prince, and I felt him trying to suck my own power from me.

"Remember your love," he hissed. "How he died for you, how you caused his destruction … "

His power, leeching off my own while mixing with his, while I was also trying to overpower him, caused a circular stream of power to flow between us, and it wound faster and faster, as I felt myself pulled back into my Star.

The world was full of brightness and light and life, and there was no void, no place where life did not touch.

I looked across the starlit universe, past all the moons and worlds and places, and there he was.

Almeisan.

We were friends, fit together to comfortable ease. I watched as we disagreed, we argued, we laughed, we loved. He loved me fervently, and I in my own heart was enraptured and overjoyed to find his love added more to my existence, even though I had not thought it possible.

"See how you loved him … " Yashool's voice whispered out to me again.

I could hardly look away. I wanted to fall into those moments on the other side of Time. I wanted to live them again. I wanted to undo everything I had done that was wrong before I'd fallen, all so I could get back to Almeisan and Adonaias.

"Adonaias," I whispered.

At that second, it barely hit me, that this was unusual.

Yashool was talking about Almeisan. In third person.

He is not Almeisan.

"You tricked me!" I yelled, furious.

I watched as the last of my former memories faded, as my power surged simultaneously with righteous and self-righteous anger.

The turbulence between us cleared, and Yashool was thrown back. The light of my power continued to burn him, and I stood up in front of him.

"You thought you could use me," I hissed, angry. "You thought you could use my friends and loved ones against me."

Yashool didn't hear me; he was screaming and writhing on the cement roof.

I held out my hand for my bow, and it came rushing into my palm. I plucked an arrow out of the air, and let its light explode with my determination.

"Your death will let the rest of them know," I whispered. "Lady Justice is back, and she has no Mercy to temper her power."

I took aim at the demon's heart of power. I felt my fingers slide back.

And then I wondered, too painfully to admit to myself at the time, if in consigning him to the void, by snuffing out his power on this side of Time, that meant I would never get to see more of Almeisan.

The thought of losing him, again, and by my own hand, caused my aim to falter.

Yashool took my arrow right in the face; I saw the spark as it burned into his mouth. The rest of my power faded from him, and he limped back from me.

"Yashool," he roared, and then he took off.

I just stood there.

So many emotions and thoughts raced through me, I could really only stand there for several long moments, trying to find a rational line of thought between it all and pull myself out of my self-entanglement.

I was angry, I was upset. I was bitter, I was lonely.

I was so stupid for letting him get away. It was okay that I let him go.

I was failing to live up to my supernatural calling. It was good enough for a first real try.

I had done the right thing. I had done the wrong thing.

There would be more trouble later. I could handle it better later.

These conflicting thoughts burrowed into me, and I burrowed even deeper into myself, retreating to the core of who I was, and blocking out all the rest.

It was the Time Tower clock that woke me up from my inner stupor.

"Ayah!" I gasped, and I looked over just in time to see her fall from her ledge, as the clock struck a new hour. "No!"

I dove off the rooftop, dropping the Bow of Righteousness and doing everything I could to make sure I saved Ayah.

My knees bled as I skidded across the sidewalk in front of the Time Tower, sliding to catch her. I felt Ayah's body crash into mine before she slipped through my hands. She rolled across the cement several times before she stopped, face up, at the edge of the street.

"No, Ayah!" I cried, and I hurried over to her, staggering with the pain in my knees. I prayed that I had cushioned her fall enough that she would live.

I picked her up and felt her heart beating irregularly. "No," I whispered, before calling up my own power.

I placed my hand on her heart and pushed my healing power into her. "Come back to me," I called, trying to get her to hear me again.

She coughed a moment later, and I nearly cheered to see her hazel eyes open, even if they were blurry and confused.

My happiness was further secured when I saw that her Soulfire was present.

"I'm so glad you're alive, Ayah," I said, before I hugged her.

She hugged me back, muttering a few questions here and there. I barely noticed how my own heart was beating quickly, as if it were in a panic.

I let her go. "How do you feel?" I asked. "Do you remember what happened?"

237

Ayah shook her head. "Who are you?"

It was the first question of hers I could fully understand and answer. I squeezed her hand. I wanted to tell her I was a friend, and in fact, I was one of her best friends. But as I watched her eyes slowly close again, I knew that I would have to find another way to answer her question. I couldn't give her my name, after all.

I nearly rolled my eyes, thinking of what that silly newswoman, Patricia whatever-her-name-was, would say.

"Raiya."

I nearly jumped as I heard my name from behind me. I relaxed only when I saw it was just Grandpa. "Grandpa," I said. "You scared me."

"We're even then," he said. "I was worried about you. I saw you fighting that demon on the roof up there." He pointed to the building where I had been only moments before, and I gulped. It suddenly seemed a lot higher than it had before.

He knelt before me, next to Ayah, who was sleeping soundly. "I'll call the ambulance for her," he said, feeling her forehead.

"Thank you." I let out a tired sigh. "I'm exhausted."

"You'll soon learn why I look as old as I do," Grandpa said with a small chortle, and I was relieved that he seemed more optimistic. My battle with Yashool had proven my ability, and I was happy for it.

I decided not to let Grandpa know that I had stopped myself from finishing him off. I didn't want to admit to Grandpa, or myself, that it was love that had stopped me in a strange way.

Part of me was worried that I would have to give that up, too, and I was already giving up so much.

"I'm proud of you," Grandpa said. "I'm really proud of you, Raiya."

"Thank you," I said.

That was really all I could say. I had not defeated the demon, but I had proven my power and my skill. I had lived up to my grandfather's expectations.

And, most importantly, I had kept my broken heart from breaking anymore. I knew I had much to atone for with my life; I had to do my duty—I had to sacrifice and work hard and keep my focus on what I truly wanted.

At that moment, I locked away my heart, determined to keep it safe and secure, and set out to do just that. While I knew I would be tested in this in the coming days and weeks and years, as I stood there, next to Grandpa, transformed, with my bow in hand, I knew I could continue on, and I knew, more importantly, that I would.

☼17☼
The Sadness of the *Starry Night*

True to his word, Grandpa called the ambulance, and Ayah was taken to the hospital. I followed at a distance.

As I walked toward the waiting room, I saw Dr. Dinger. I don't think he was surprised to see me outside their hallway. He glanced at me, and only nodded quietly.

Soon after that, I began offering him more blood samples. I never asked him what he did with the samples, and I thought this was a fair deal. I assumed he did some research on it, and I didn't mind, as long as I didn't know the specifics.

I decided not to ask what the Skarmastad Foundation might be doing with my blood; it seemed like too much of a hassle to worry about, when I had more demons and my heart and my semblance of a life to focus on.

In my own way, I knew I was trying to save what we had before, but it was too late.

The once easy grace of his companionship waned, and even though I still respected him, our bond seemed to fade along with the rest of my friendships.

Jeff and Chelsea needed a few days to recover, but I was glad to see that each of them had their Soulfire returned, and everything was back to normal for them. Ayah needed a good week in the hospital for her injuries from the Time Tower.

I managed to take the coward's way out there; I didn't go see them. I didn't talk to them, I didn't call to see how they

240

were doing, and I didn't seek them out once they were back in school. I listened through the gossip lines at school, but that was all I allowed myself to do.

I figured it was an easy way of convincing them I no longer cared about them, and I no longer cared for our friendship. When I thought about it, I decided it complemented my previous attempts to sever our ties nicely.

I would have taken the coward's way out with Reggie, too, and avoided him as well—if only he would've let me.

He'd been gone from school for so long, I was surprised when he came up to me in art class on the following Monday morning.

"Hey, Raiya," he said, greeting me with an easy smile as he pushed the art room's supply cart out into the hall and parked it in front of the mural. "*Starry Night* is really looking good, I think."

I felt my head start to spin with fear. "I didn't know you were back."

Reggie laughed. "Yeah, it's been a while, huh?" He glanced down at the cart. "I thought I'd bring this to you, so you can finish up the mural."

"Just me?" The words seemed clogged in my throat.

"Yeah. I've decided I'm not going to work on the mural anymore."

I could almost hear the "with you" he'd withheld. "Why?" I asked.

"Well, I talked to Ms. Carmichael this morning, and because I'm behind in all my classes," he said as he rolled his eyes, "I'm going to drop out of art this semester."

"But you love it," I said, surprised how offended I felt by his decision. I knew I'd broken his heart, but that was no reason for him to let go of his own heart's pursuit.

He shook his head. "It's alright," he said. "Just because I'm not in class doesn't mean I'm giving up on it. I'm just giving up on the grade for it."

"Oh." I didn't really know what else to say. "So this is your last class?"

"Well, I wanted to talk to you, actually," he said. "I'm supposed to be in another class right now."

I backed away from him, grabbing my palette and several brushes. I knew I could distract myself from the upcoming discomfort, and so I would.

It was for the best. I didn't want to end up hurting him—or trying to stop myself from hurting him—again.

"What did you want to talk about?" I asked, as I began to paint the hole where I'd punched right through the cement. Ms. Carmichael told me that they would worry about fixing it later on, when next year's budget came through. In the meantime, I decided to try to paint it in such a way that it didn't seem like a real hole. It was really the least I could do, considering I was the one behind the damage.

"I wanna talk about what happened," he said, and my paintbrush almost fell from my fingers again. I tightened my grip at once, briefly thinking of my new bow. It was a weapon against the supernatural evil that still haunted me; in some ways, the paintbrush almost felt like a weapon, too. Or maybe it was really more of a shield.

"Well, talk then," I remarked to Reggie, determined to carry on the pretense of being normal.

"I wasn't really sure what happened," he began. "And the doctors couldn't really tell me either. And neither could my family."

I nodded. "I can't really tell you what happened either."

Right there, I made a vow that I would never tell him what actually happened, and I would never tell anyone anything I didn't want to ever again, either. If my supernatural power was truly mine to bear alone, then I would choose which elements to inflict on other people, and I would not feel sorry for doing so.

"I figured," he said. He leaned against the dry building some. "My parents couldn't tell me anything about me, but my dad had quite a story for me when I woke up."

"Story?" I asked.

"Yeah. Maybe you even saw it on the news? The *Mirror* picked it up," he said. "My dad was caught in a building collapse at the site where he was working. There was a fire and then a flood. It was a miracle he survived."

"Oh. I'm glad he did," I said, but I felt the heat start to creep out from under my collar.

"He told me that there was an angel who saved him," Reggie said. "An angel with white wings and weapons of light, with purple eyes."

I nervously batted at my own hair, trying to make it look like I was shoving it out of my own eyes, but really I was trying to hide further from the world.

"Oh," I said again. "That sounds weird. But I'm glad he's okay."

"Me, too," Reggie said. "But the story gets weirder."

"It does?" I began to feel panic rise inside of me. And then a battle with myself ensued, as I firmly told myself it was time to grow up, get a backbone, and cut ties with Reggie. I didn't owe him the truth. He couldn't force it out of me. And it wasn't like he would be able to prove anything.

"I went to visit Ayah," he said. He gave me a small smile. "You were right about her, by the way."

"She did like you," I murmured.

"Yeah, you can just say 'I told ya so,'" Reggie replied, grinning. "I know you want to."

I did, but I only smiled instead. "So she admitted it to you?"

"Yeah," he said. "It was a very nice visit."

From the way he said it, I had a feeling it was a very nice visit indeed, but I didn't press for details. It was enough to know that Ayah was happy.

"I guess Ayah's doing better then?"

"Yeah, she is. But the funny part about her is that she had a story about an angel hero, too," he said.

Everything went hot and cold at the same time. My face flushed over, while I felt chills run down my spine.

I tried to cover up my discomfort by focusing intently on my painting. "That's weird," I finally said, a long moment later.

"Yeah," Reggie agreed. "I thought so, too, Raiya."

Our eyes met for a long moment, and I realized he suspected something.

"I think there's more to the story than what I've been told," he said, his voice careful and precise.

I shrugged. "There probably is," I said slowly. "But there are always some mysteries about these things, right?"

Reggie sighed, before he turned to face the mural. "You know," he said, "I thought it was weird that you picked this, at the beginning of school. But I get it now."

"Get what?"

"Vincent van Gogh painted this scene here, and it's a take on what he saw outside his asylum," Reggie said. "People said that he made an idealized village, and some others speculate that it was a sort of longing for heaven that compelled him."

The Celestial Kingdom brushed past my mind, the concept of home too grand for me to properly contemplate inside my mind.

"He never sold a painting in his life, and he felt that his life was one of only constant suffering," Reggie said. "His last words were 'The sadness will last forever.'"

I looked back at the mural of *Starry Night*, my humble attempt to capture the original's energetic rush of peace and paralyzing emotion, that moment of stillness that offered up no hope but still sought to find it.

"Are you saying that I should spend more time in an asylum, looking out a window?" I asked, keeping my tone light with levity.

"No." He gave me a rueful smile. "I just meant that *Starry Night* is something important to you, because it's proof to you, whether you know the full story behind it or not, that beauty can come from the longest and deepest sort of suffering."

Another level of appreciation for van Gogh's works rushed through me, and I nodded. "Maybe you're right."

"It's still a bit of a mystery, especially with that idealized village," he said. "So I guess it's not as different from your other work as I thought it was."

I said nothing to that. It was so easy to say nothing.

"As for my own mystery, about my story, I think I know enough that it helps other things make sense. And maybe the mystery even adds more to the beauty."

Sighing, I turned away. "Maybe one day you'll figure the rest out," I said. I put my palette and paintbrushes down, and walked over to him. "But, in the meantime, I owe you an apology. For what happened. I know we can't be the same friends we were before, but I hope you know, that whatever happens, I'll always be grateful for the time we did have together."

Reggie's face fell into a sad frown, but he shrugged a moment later.

"I guess I should have known you didn't feel that way about me," he said. He glanced back at the mural. "You're in love with someone else."

The crystal blue eyes swam into my memory, and I had to wonder if Reggie had seen the messy streaks where I'd mindlessly painted that face.

"What makes you think that?" I asked, my voice barely a whisper.

"Your paintings," he said. "I know your work very well, Raiya. I can see it in your work. You've been drawing someone for a long time with too much care and too much uncertainty for me not to see how much you love him, whoever he is."

I thought of that night, that one after I'd transformed and saved Reggie's dad and some of his coworkers. I'd gone back to my room, where my artwork hung, some of it finished and painted, others half-sketched.

I remembered how the room had lit up, as they were all colored with new meaning and old memories. The Phoenix Star, the Star of Mercy who had been born from the ashes of the Star of Fire—Almeisan.

He's right. Reggie's right. I can't believe it, but he's right.

Almeisan.

I did love him.

And I had destroyed him, too, apparently.

I thought of Yashool, and then quickly turned away.

"I don't want to talk about it anymore," I snapped. "I don't want you to talk about it anymore, either, frankly."

"You don't have to be so blunt about it."

I only softened a little at his sadness. I guess, from his standpoint, I'd more or less admitted he was right.

And he was, really.

"Sorry."

"It's alright," he told me softly. He titled his head at me a little, giving me a kind but quizzical smile. "But I have to admit, I'm a little surprised at your choice. To stay away from me and the others, I mean."

THE STARLIGHT CHRONICLES

"Why?" I scrunched up my nose, a little irritated. "I'm only going to hurt you more if we stay friends. I mean, really, unrequited love and crushes ruin things. So you should know why I'd rather not pretend everything is the same as before. I'm not the same as before, either."

"I know." He sighed. "It's just … you can't escape pain in this life, Raiya. And not all pain is bad pain. I thought you knew that."

"I *do* know that," I growled.

"Then you should know, while I wouldn't have enjoyed the pain you would cause me, I would have gladly bourn it, if it meant we could still be friends."

His voice was a little more rough, and I was glad for it. I think that was the only reason why I still shook my head. "Well, I don't want to deal with it. But I'm sorry I'm not as strong as you are."

Reggie nodded. "I understand." He held out his hand for mine, and I took it.

I allowed myself a full moment, a lasting moment, to enjoy the feel of his hands against mine, to watch as we gripped each other tightly with our overlapping fingers. I squeezed him tightly, and then let him go.

I'd already mourned his loss, and I was ready to let him go, even if my body said otherwise. My fingers felt like they were broken as the last of his touch slipped away.

THE STARLIGHT CHRONICLES

Reggie tucked his hands into his pockets. "Well," he said. "I think I'll leave you to *Starry Night* then, huh?"

I nodded, stuffing my tears back into my head.

Before I could stop him, he leaned in and gave me a quick kiss on the cheek. It was only a small peck, a whisper of lips against my skin.

"Thank you," he whispered.

I let the warmth of his affection wash over me, as Reggie then turned and walked away.

Moments passed, and then the bell rang. I looked back up at the mural before me. It wasn't too far from being finished, although it wasn't going to be complete before the school's open house. Ms. Carmichael would be disappointed, especially hearing that Reggie was going to step away from the project.

I reached up and placed my hand over the hole in the wall, letting my fingers drift lightly over the half-dried paint.

"The sadness will last forever," I whispered.

As I packed up my things and headed out to my next class, I couldn't help but think how appropriate that was.

Years later, I would return to that idea, to that moment. I didn't know it, as Reggie walked away, but that was when my superhero name began to form in the subconscious part of my mind.

Maybe it wasn't just the name that was conceived at that time. In many ways, at that moment, as I swept the last pieces of my broken heart aside, Starry Knight was born.

☼18☼
The Consequences of Losing Control—Part 2

So that's how everything was ruined.

Everything about my life—as already complicated as it was, as already unusual as it was—was ruined, shortly after I started seventh grade.

Some people worry that hormones will be the death of them. Supernatural calling was the death of me, and I knew that death, that dying to my own selfish desires, as unselfish as they might have been, was only the first death I would experience.

After the talk with Reggie, I was able to see my destiny more clearly than ever, and I was able to shake off everything that would hold me back, everything that could stop me.

And eventually, everything was alright.

Eventually.

But still, sometimes, even though everything is ruined, people forget that that can still be a good thing. My friendships were gone and over, but my friends were safe. Or at least, they were safer. After Ayah's near-death experience, there were some personal demons that came around, but I was able to shut them up and shut them down much more quickly.

Yashool would make another appearance every once in a while, but he always managed to slither away from me before

I could destroy him. I let him stay, in many ways, even though we were enemies.

Life became much easier when Jeff moved down to Florida just before Thanksgiving that year, and Chelsea began taking extra advanced classes. By the time I caught up on all the school I missed, which was a lot over the next couple of years, I was nearly a full grade behind her. Despite our differences, and our tepid, tragic parting, we were simply polite to each other. I was never sure if she forgave me or not.

As for Ayah, her dad's consultation firm transferred him to New York City a few months later. Reggie's parents actually followed them, since Reggie's dad was offered a job to help build the new building headquarters for Ayah's dad. I was really happy for Tomas, since I knew he wanted a shot at a second chance to design something that would last, especially after the construction project for the underground lab at Lake Erie fell through.

Jeff and I lost contact, as I'd predicted at the beginning. It wasn't until nearly two decades later that I would learn through the Rosemont alumni newsletter that he was still writing music, all while juggling a family and a teaching job.

Chelsea became a head engineer for a software and web company. She finally moved into her dream house and never invited her family over, unless it was a holiday and someone else was cooking. She got a lot of cats and only lived life on her terms.

Ayah went to a prestigious college, and ended up designing her own special fashion line. She went to work for another big company, who bought her designs. I lost track of her after that. In all fairness, her company sent her all over the world, so I think that was easy enough to be confused about.

And as for Reggie …

The day that Reggie came to see me about the mural was the last day we ever talked. I heard about him through the gossip lines after that.

I was actually fine with that. I knew we parted on good terms, and after everything that happened—twisting his Soulfire up in Time's fabric, dumping his friendship and offer for more than friendship, and dismissing all the years of kindness as nothing to fight for—I was so, so grateful for just that.

Reggie moved to New York City with his family and became a big street artist. He has a new name, just as he promised me all those years ago, and I can assure you it's an even better one than Starry Knight.

I never thought about it until later, but eventually, I was actually glad that everything happened the way it did.

It's hard to be grateful for things, especially painful things. But it was true that I would have never released the fabric of

254

Time if Reggie hadn't been such a good friend to me, I wouldn't have let go of my friends if nothing else had happened, and I wouldn't have been as prepared as I was for the fulfillment of my mission as the fallen Star of Justice. Worse still, I might have ended up risking their lives for our friendship, and I would have added to my list of sins, the ones I would never forgive myself for, had something indeed happened to them.

I think of them still, every once in a while, and I wish them all the best as I sit there and remember them.

Sometimes, people are too precious to hold onto. Those times, we can only keep them in our prayers, in our thoughts, in our dreams. For me, I could even keep them close through my paintings.

That was enough, I told myself.

It had to be enough.

For years, I did not allow my heart to voice its disagreement. I knew I had a broken heart, and because of that, I knew I was lost. But even as I knew I was lost, I found that I deserved it in the end.

And even when I could tell my heart was stewing silently, angry at me and angry at the world, I ran through the list of reasons why it was better to keep my duty separate from my heart, and why my heart should only be content for what the other side of Time had waiting for me.

It worked.

THE STARLIGHT CHRONICLES

Over the next few years, as demons came—more slowly than expected, even if they were just as clever—I fought them in shadow, defeating them in swift silence. Grandpa congratulated me when I succeeded, and helped me when, like with Yashool, I found myself too hesitant to strike back and go for the kill. I worked hard to rectify my slipups, and I prepared for the day when I would meet my sisters face-to-face once more.

Other things happened, too.

Grandpa eased up on my training some, seeing how competently I managed the small demons and monsters that came to Apollo City.

Rachel finished college, with good marks, and I watched as she fell ever more deeply in love with Lee, and together they transformed our house into Rachel's dream coffee shop. During her grand opening, shortly after the small crowd in attendance cheered at the unveiling of "Rachel's Café," Lee proposed and Rachel said yes. I was immediately conscripted to be the maid of honor, and Lee's brother, Logan, was introduced as his best man.

Rachel tried to get me to go on a few dates with him, and it was a friendly sort of awkward. In many ways, I considered Lee and Logan more like my own brothers, now that Rachel was going to marry Lee.

It was nice.

And it was pretty funny, watching Aunt Letty fume at the thought of having to find a wedding date.

So there was plenty to do, helping out Rachel, working on my school work, often with Grandpa's help, especially as we began to read more classics, and making sure I kept my supernatural self focused and ready for the day when the Sinisters would appear again.

I also kept up my appointments with Dr. Dinger. My broken heart was still broken, but I was able to see that there was a lot of good I could do with it in the meantime. It was good to know I could still add to the beauty while I was here, for however long it might end up being.

So things were okay.

Everything was going along fine. Everything was nearly perfect, even.

Everything, of course, until the day when everything was ruined.

Again.

I went through the motions of a busy life for so long they became a part of me, as if I was training myself to be a robot or a zombie—somebody who wasn't allowed to feel things the way humans did, who wasn't allowed to get excited or anxious or be afraid, someone who wasn't allowed to fail, someone who wasn't allowed to fall in love—as much as I was refining my skill as a Starlight Warrior.

257

It was that last part that led to all the others.

I fell in love.

I didn't mean to fall in love.

Even after I did, I fought against it for months, before I accepted it, and it took several months more before I allowed myself to embrace a resolution, to let myself pretend I had earned the right to choose the fate my heart was unable to ignore.

But I will never, ever forget the moment that I felt my heart choose to break free from the detached prison inside of me.

Just a little over three years after I lost all my friends, the year I started in tenth grade, I found myself in Apollo Central High School, the home of my school's longtime sports rivals. I was a little surprised, and yet not surprised, to find myself there. At Rachel's insistence, and even out of my own conceded boredom, I was working on the set design for a play production with Ms. Carmichael and some of our other art students. (Ms. Carmichael had been promoted to the sophomore and junior level classes the same year I began tenth grade.) I was not excited about being there, but Ms. Carmichael knew me well enough to know how to fix that.

"Raiya," Ms. Carmichael called. "You're going to work on painting the backdrop."

I grinned despite myself. "Okay."

Beside me, Courtney pouted. "Why do you give her all the good jobs? Don't you remember the last time you did?"

I winced at her words. From the look on Ms. Carmichael's face, we all knew what Courtney was referring to.

It was time to distract her. "Come on, Courtney," I said with a sneer, "Ms. Carmichael knows you're better suited to the building sets. Besides, you can flirt more easily with some of the guys around here. I'll just be painting at the back of the stage."

Courtney scowled. "As if," she muttered. "There are only a couple of them that are worth it, and they seem content to goof off."

She gestured toward the back of the stage area, where there were several people gathered. I recognized some of them, from my previous visits, while there were a few new faces among them.

"*Romeo and Juliet* is for a more civilized age," I agreed softly, watching as the one boy began carrying the other on his back and turning in circles. Another one came up behind them and laughed, before telling them something that made them stop.

He was probably laughing at them, I thought. I scowled, as I realized one of them had my art case. And then I took a deep breath and let it go.

There were a lot of stories about the silliness of the Apollo Central students, compared to the Rosemont students, anyway. Rosemont was a school that took our work seriously, and our pride in that work even more seriously. Our football team went up against Central and won more often than not because we were the better trained team, even if we were not always the better prepared.

259

From the few weeks of helping out at the play practice, I didn't see much that would counter that kind of reputation.

One of the girls standing next to them suddenly waved to me. I smiled and waved back politely. Gwen Kessler was one of the people from Central who had really made an effort to make the Rosemont students feel welcome, and I found no fault with her. She was a lovely girl, perfect for the role of Juliet.

Before too long, I got to work. I noticed that Chelsea had come along with us, using it as one of her extracurricular activities for her early college application. We were polite to each other, and that was it. I was grateful for this, even though I was saddened, too.

I suppose by now I should be used to it, I reminded myself. I shuffled my feelings to the side and began to work on the backdrop.

It was a night sky, and I smiled as I worked, recalling how I'd finished the mural outside of Ms. Carmichael's class in seventh grade. I had added a lot more of my work to my personal collection since then, but there was something, I had to admit, about painting a night sky.

Many people would have been content to leave it at blue and add in some stars. I might have even made it similar to van Gogh's *Starry Night* painting, just to make it even more of an inside joke with myself.

I glanced over at my art case. Since seventh grade, I had not only added to my collection of artwork, but my art supplies as

THE STARLIGHT CHRONICLES

well. Just in time for the new school year, Rachel had given me a new case, one that had a lot more room for supplies.

But I was already out of orange, I noticed.

"What is it, Raiya?" Chelsea asked. "Do you need something?"

I turned to see her standing behind me. "I need an orange," I said, keeping it simple. "Can you, um, get me some, please? And maybe a new brush, too?"

"Sure." Her tone was bracingly polite, and I had to wonder if she wasn't a little upset at herself, considering she did talk to me if she could help it anymore.

Chelsea hurried off, and I turned my attention back to the painting, even though my heart briefly ached. I squashed it down again, reprimanding it softly, like a dog who has learned its lessons too well.

I did start with some blue, letting it fade from black to blue to violet to a mix of rose and orange. It would be a bright, grand sky, I decided, and I worked to make it come together, blending the different colors perfectly.

I had the background colors in place drying when I heard another person approach me from behind. "This is awful," Courtney told me.

"It's not done yet," I told her, standing up. I had a few spots of paint on me, some smudges running down my Rosemont socks and my skirt.

Courtney frowned. "Well, at least let me help you, since I'm done with my work," she said.

"No, thank you," I said, much as I had in seventh grade. I stepped in front of her, protecting my work. "I'm good."

"But I'm not doing anything, and neither are you."

"I'm waiting for the paint to dry, and then I'll add on the top layers."

"God, you're so annoying," Courtney hissed. "All I want to do is help."

"No," I said. "No, all you want is to look good. I can prove it to you."

"Oh, really?" Courtney crossed her arms over her chest.

"Yes. Here." I handed her some of my paintbrushes, some of them still dripping with paint. "If you want to help, you can go and clean these for Ms. Carmichael."

"Ew, gross," Courtney moaned.

"Take them," I said again, waving them at her.

"No!" Courtney stepped back quickly, just barely making it out of the way.

I looked down at the paintbrushes, following the little line of paint dots that now littered the stage. "See?" I said. "You don't want to help. You just want the glory."

Courtney huffed disgustedly. "You think you're so clever, Raiya," she spat. "But you're just a snob and no one likes you.

262

Thank God I'm smart enough not to be your friend. Oh, wait, *everyone is,* because you don't have any!"

Her words hit me like a slap. But I was used to that. The worst part was my own self-inflicted pain. As long as it had been, and as terrible as everything had been between us, I still waited to hear Chelsea come up running beside me, to defend me.

She didn't come.

Which was fair and good, I reminded myself. I was about to go and clean my own paintbrushes when Courtney tripped over one of the stage hand's paint buckets. She screamed and hollered about her new shoes, and I could honestly say nothing.

I had to wonder if Adonaias had worked some of his own power. In the many years since seventh grade, he had become more known to me, and I had to wonder if he'd been trying to get a laugh out of me, or if he was trying to comfort me, or if he was simply showing Courtney she was wrong. Maybe it was even some combination of all three of those things, and I was grateful for it.

Still, I stifled the laughter and went back to work. There's nothing honorable about enjoying an enemy's defeat. That's not where my victory would come from, and I knew that.

"Still have to clean those paintbrushes," I murmured to myself, before heading out to one of the sinks outside of the auditorium.

Despite Courtney's interruption of my work, it really was nothing out of the ordinary.

I could handle her outbursts. After all these years sharing art class together, I knew what to expect from her. Still, I did a careful walk through the auditorium and the stage area, taking the long way back to my work, hoping I did not run into Yashool or any other demon monster hoping to steal some souls. I knew if I had been one of them, Courtney would have been a good candidate. Her Soulfire was dotted with a mix of pretty lights, but there were plenty of hollow spots as well.

Nothing out of the ordinary.

But then something happened that I never would have expected.

I came back to the stage with my cleaned paintbrushes in my hand. I scooted toward the curtain, so the set designers could finish moving Courtney's painted balcony to its proper place. As I passed by, I couldn't help but notice several of her strokes were hurried and slapdash; Ms. Carmichael would likely ask her to redo some of it. But I had to wonder if the paint had something to do with it, too; it looked a little runny, as though the school had watered it down in order to have more of it.

I hope none of my work has that, I thought with a sigh.

I turned back to look at the backdrop.

And there he was.

THE STARLIGHT CHRONICLES

There was a boy who was seated on my work, looking over the design. I stopped in my tracks as I saw him. If this had been any normal situation—even one of my new normal situations—I would have been upset he was sitting onto of the backdrop at all. It looked like he'd tripped, but I didn't see any skid marks in the drying paint, so everything was okay with the painting.

Normally, I would have been tempted to tell him to get off, to move, to stop touching my stuff. And I was just about to do so, too.

But in that second, I saw it.

His Soulfire glimmered at me, and I felt it was too incredible to believe it.

And then he spoke. "Wow," he said. "That's really good."

Almeisan.

My eyes teared up for the first time in months. I felt my legs go numb. The clean paintbrushes fell out of my hands.

The boy glanced over toward me, no doubt surprised by the sound.

I ducked into the shadows even further, still too overwhelmed to do anything else. I felt my breath catch in my throat, terrified he would see me, and even more terrified he would recognize me.

"Huh … " He shrugged.

For the briefest second, I saw his eyes.

265

Cool, crystalline blue. They were the eyes of the Star in my painting, the ones from my memory. It was him.

It has to be him.

"No," I moaned, as my heart broke through the cage I'd placed it in. I felt it slip out of its own accord, and even as I fought the reality of what I was seeing and feeling and experiencing, boundless joy enraptured me.

I fought back harder. "No," I said again. "No, it can't be him."

Yashool had to be there, I thought, even though I had just made sure there was nothing around. But he had to be there, I figured. Playing the cruelest joke on me possible.

I watched as the detention bell rang, and the boy suddenly jumped up.

"Woo-hoo!" he cheered. "Freedom! Time to get out of here."

Yes, I thought. *This has to be a joke. This has to be a demon trick. Or something like that.*

I glanced down at my wrist. Nothing. No pain, no humming, no signal to let me know there was a monster nearby.

Nothing.

As the boy left, I crept out from behind the curtain, keeping watch over him.

THE STARLIGHT CHRONICLES

It was too much for me to believe. But I couldn't help but believe it. My thoughts all seemed to whirl around and then hit me forcefully, washing over me like ripples across the lake water.

He's alive.

He is alive.

He is really alive.

Almeisan is alive.

As he exited the auditorium, calling out his goodbyes to Gwen and his other friends—all loudly, with that cringe-worthy element of popularity and self-importance that I absolutely hated—I felt the world around me spin, shifting faster and slower, and then more dangerously than ever.

My heart felt alive again, and I couldn't stand the thought of never seeing that boy again, even as I dreaded it.

I would try to talk myself out of believing it was him, and for a while, I succeeded. But eventually, my heart demanded I respond.

So once more, everything—all my plans, all my preparation, all my intentions and work—*everything* was ruined, and it was all ruined by love.

☼Epilogue☼
A Starlight Legacy of Love

As I finish my story, I watch as my daughter's eyes light up with laughter. She chuckles at the absurdity, even though I know she's heard the story at least a thousand times.

When her laughter quiets down, she looks at me with her own blue-violet eyes. "Mom," she begins, "is that how I'll know if I fall in love for real? I'll just know?"

"I don't know," I admit. "Love is a strange thing sometimes. Even when we think we've got it all figured out, there's still something to discover about it."

"So I'll never be sure?"

"You can be sure of your own heart's promise to be there for the one you love, my lovely Lyra," I say. "In this world, it's only action that we can objectively see."

She contemplates this for a while, and I feel surprise at seeing how much she has grown over the years. Her own Starlight power, as I see it, has grown along with her, and I suddenly ache for the days when she was a little girl.

I pat her hand in a motherly manner, making her smile. "You know I'll always be here to help you," I assure her. "So there's my love you can depend on. And your father's, too."

At this, Lyra laughs. "Daddy was a real ham when you first met him, huh?" she says, using one of our oldest jokes.

"What do you mean, 'was?'" I ask, narrowing my eyes playfully at the door. A small skirmish proves my hunch correct; my beloved was lurking around the door. "Do you want to come in here and take a bow?" I call out.

I get the answer I'm expecting.

"I think I will, since it's clear you went through all that effort just to make me the star," Hamilton replies, as he pokes his head into Lyra's bedroom.

"I knew you were there," I tell him, knowing there's no chance of disappointing him over that.

He gives Lyra a deep bow, and Lyra, even in the midst of her teenage years, still laughs as her father and I joke around with each other.

He winks at me. "I knew you knew," he replies. "That's why I stayed."

I could argue some more, but I give up; I am more helpless than I'll ever admit when it comes to Hamilton. I fell in love with him several times, but I never seemed to fall enough to satisfy my heart. Each morning since we'd married seemed to only bring more reasons for me to fall into him, and I never seem to grow tired of holding onto him as we fall together.

I stand up and move to kiss his cheek; instantly, he gives me that same old smirk of his and tilts his face, and I end up kissing him on the mouth instead.

Lyra sighs on her bed behind us. "You guys are insufferable," she mutters.

Hamilton and I laugh and then kiss each other again, just to make sure she appreciates just how insufferable we really are.

"You guys! Ew, gross, get out of my room." Lyra shoots up off her bed and pushes at us both. We're out of her room less than a second before she slams the door after us.

Hamilton reminds her that we own the house, but I just curl up in the small nook of his shoulder. "She's a teenager," I say.

"Are you suggesting that we have more children?" Hamilton asks. He cocks an eyebrow at me, playful and hopeful at the same time.

"No," I reply. "I just meant she's right to be disturbed at our affection."

"Well, considering our past, we should consider it an admirable goal to make our kids uncomfortable with how much we love each other," he says, and I hold onto him more tightly.

"I'll work on that," I murmured into his collarbone, gratified by his insight. He definitely had his moments, both good and bad, but I always loved it when he gave me something good to hold onto. The idea of subjecting Lyra and Lucas to a large amount of our romantic and playful banter makes me smile as much as it humbles me.

"What's wrong?" he asks, sensing my seriousness. "Come on, Raiya, I know you enjoy the story of how you fell in love with me. I've heard you tell it for years now."

"I know," I say. "I do love it. I was actually more worried for Lyra."

"Why?" Instantly, there's a hint of horrified suspicion in those deep blue eyes. "She fall in love with someone already?"

"I don't know for sure," I say honestly. "She has been skirting around the topic when I ask her about her friends lately, especially when I ask her about love. I think there's a boy who's caught her attention."

"Boy trouble already?" Hamilton laments. "Now I know for sure I'm getting old."

"Age is nothing in eternity, my love." I laugh at him, and he sticks his tongue out at me. He was vain in some of the smallest ways, but I still loved him for it. "But either way, you have to admit, we've set the stakes pretty high for her."

"She's our daughter," Hamilton insists. "High standards, high stakes, high expectations. It's part of the family genes."

I laugh again. "Maybe I should have sent you in," I muse thoughtfully. "She asked me how I knew for sure you were the one I was meant to be with. Not everyone gets the supernatural help we do."

Hamilton cupped my cheeks. "We still have to choose it," he says, before he kisses me again. "That's what you taught me, remember? It's something that chooses you, and you get to choose back."

"I thought you learned that from the Prince."

He shrugs. "I can learn the same lesson in different contexts in different ways."

"You mean you had to learn something more than once?" I tease.

"Shut up," he says, rolling his eyes. But he looks at me with a softer glance and adds, "You know I would sit through the same lessons over and over and over again, as long as it means I get you in the end."

I think of all the loss I had endured over the years, and for only a second I wonder if I would do it all again, knowing I would be with Hamilton in the end. My pain was not an easy thing to let go of, and I did not minimalize it or trivialize it as I weighed the scenario in my mind.

But I have to admit, as much as I might have hated it, that Hamilton was right. I decide not to tell him that part as I agree with him.

"I would too."

He lifts me up and cradles me to his chest. As I begin to protest, he kisses me. "People don't need to be taught so often as they need to be reminded. And for you, it will be *my pleasure* to remind you of that now."

Lyra groans from behind her door, and I briefly hear Lucas as he pokes his head out of the living room down the hall. "What's wrong?" he asks.

THE STARLIGHT CHRONICLES

"Mom and Dad are being lovey-dovey *again*," Lyra yells at him, but I ignore it as I allow my husband to literally sweep me off my feet.

"I wonder if happily-ever-afters are also something you get to choose," I murmur, as we head toward our room.

"No," Hamilton says. "No, I'm pretty sure you have to work for those."

"Maybe it's gift," I say, "since we don't deserve it."

"Maybe it's a bit of both." He shrugs. "Either way, I know I have mine."

As he kisses me again, I have no doubt of his joy, and I have no doubt of my own heart. All the brokenness washes away, and I am left with the music and light of true love inside of me.

C. S. Johnson is the author of several young adult novels, including sci-fi and fantasy adventures such as *The Starlight Chronicles* series, the *Once Upon a Princess* saga, and the *Divine Space Pirates* trilogy. With a gift for sarcasm and an apologetic heart, she currently lives in Atlanta with her family.

THANK YOU FOR PICKING UP THIS BOOK!

To Get *Awakening* (A Special Christmas Episode of The *Starlight Chronicles*) for Free,

Download It At:

https://www.csjohnson.me/awakening

THE STARLIGHT CHRONICLES

AUTHOR'S NOTE (AGAIN)

Dear Reader,

In the other books of the Starlight Chronicles, I talk of how the books reflect the believer's journey, about how life and faith often overlap and fold into each other to create something greater than just real life. Hamilton's journey throughout that series is unique, and whether you have found yourself too much like him or too little, there is no doubt that Raiya's journey throughout the series is very different from his.

While Hamilton is more like me in temperament than I would like, I actually identify more with Raiya when it comes to the beginning of my believer's journey. Just as she struggled to learn and still awe in wonder, so did (do) I grapple with the often complementary bliss and battles of faith in my heart, my head, and my habits.

I became a Christian at a very young age, and I grew up in church. I remember hearing about God in church long before I met God in a story. But I wanted to believe, and at a very young, innocent age, I did just that.

In my innocence—precious as it is, for its rarity as much as its brevity—I did not realize the truth about evil in the world. It became harder, with age and experience and awareness, to believe so simply that goodness was eternal, and even more so that it was possible. C. S. Lewis says in *Mere Christianity* that faith is something that is both easier and harder. As I grew up and grounded myself more firmly in the Word, I learned very quickly that there is armor for every age, and virtue often comes at great cost.

I hated taking those costs.

277

Like Starry Knight, I told myself duty was more important than love, rather than duty is only possible because of love. In my beginning, I shut my heart out to many because of the fear of getting hurt and losing focus on my calling.

And also like Starry Knight, it was not so long after I declared I would do my duty to the world and keep my heart to myself that my heart fell free of its own accord. My husband's faithfulness—that often innocent sort of longing, in its own way—gave me the courage to let my mind and will follow after. I think that is a lesson God will have to teach me over and over and over and likely over again: There is no surrendering your will without giving up your heart.

I hope you have enjoyed this book, just like all the others. Please continue with the rest of the series. If you are here because you've already finished, I pray you will read through the books again—believe me, reading through knowing who is who and why who is doing what only makes it even more hilarious and poignant.

I hope to see you again in my other books as well. It is always a lovely feeling to find familiar eyes on the other side of my work.

Until We Meet Again,

C. S. Johnson

P. S. Please read on for a sample of *Slumbering*, Book 1 of The Starlight Chronicles, where you get to read Hamilton Dinger's side of the story.

Sample Reading *from*

SLUMBERING

BOOK ONE of *THE STARLIGHT CHRONICLES*

C. S. Johnson

THE STARLIGHT CHRONICLES

☼Prologue☼
Wingdinger

The winter winds were cold and harsh, laced with particles of hail and snow. The air was dry, the sun was hidden, and just from looking at it, I could tell Lake Erie was in the freezing temperatures. Apollo City, along with the rest of northern Ohio, was covered in a blanket of gray-white snow/slush, but city inhabitants were still trying to go about their humdrum lives with as little interruption as possible.

I had to say, the *eela*—shadow monster—rampaging all around the city wasn't helping. Not in the least, if you can imagine it.

As he hovered in midair, today's choice of monster giggled as he began attacking another crowd of people. He'd shown up a few times this past week, but this was the first time I'd gotten close to killing him without breaking curfew or skipping class.

Not that I minded those things, of course; I just minded getting in trouble for them.

This sinister-ling is Daikan. He "specializes" in cruel humor, but not the kind I liked or agreed with; some of his material was *really* lame. He'd been nicknamed "The Jester" by the local press—anything to get sales up without infringing on Batman's legal rights.

While he certainly reminded me of some kind of ex-con carny, there was a villainous twinkle in his eye all too reminiscent of his many demon predecessors and his fearless Sinister leaders. Not to mention there was the same cringe-worthy delusion laced in his laughter.

"Ha-ha, I told you I would have you rolling with delight sooner or later," he cried out mockingly, as indeed, the crowds rolled over, though in pain. "Daikan always has a trick up his sleeve!"

Who knew who he thought he was talking to? Some people were snapping photos, while others were running away screaming. All of this chaos was happening, of course, while I was attempting to destroy him.

Unfortunately, this was nothing out of the ordinary. It was just a typical day in the life of the superhero known as "Wingdinger." Me.

My fingers gave an icy snap as I clenched my fists. "No one's laughing down here," I retorted angrily.

Just so you know, I had a right to be angry. Daikan had largely ignored me that day, and only paid attention long enough to laugh at me. And the third-person referencing was getting old.

"Watch your back, kid," Elysian, my "pet" changeling dragon, thundered at me. He swooped down and curled protectively around me just as Daikan slashed out his attack.

Spindles of power trickled through the sky, swiping over us as Elysian ducked and I dodged. There was a sudden break as a nearby tree fell and I heard something—probably one of the old city park buildings—crumbling behind us.

"Let's go," Elysian muttered, ignoring the glare I gave him

as he leaned down to let me up on his back. But I, reluctantly, climbed on.

I wanted nothing more than to fly on my own two, irritatingly useless, wings.

As Elysian took flight, the wind bit at my face, matching the bite in my tone. "Look who's laughing now!" I taunted, tackling the laughing trickster right out of the air. Something puffy and squishy gooped through my gloves as I no doubt punched through a lung, knocking the wind (along with other substances) out of his body.

"Ugh ... Gross." If only this were some kind of video game, I thought ruefully. *Me and the guys would be all over it.*

A split second later, I was thrust back into the fight. Several events blurred through my mind as the end of the battle became eminent.

Flinging the pus off of my fist ...

Elysian's brief approving sneer ...

Falling from the sky, tangled up with the demon body ...

Ah, the welcoming rush of adrenaline. I'd become quite the junkie since this started.

I grinned to myself; I liked this trick. After several months of fighting off these monsters, I no longer had any fear of falling.

Instead of freaking out like I used to, I clawed my way on top of the evil *eela*, forcing my enemy down even more as we slammed into the ground.

Jolted but still standing, I victoriously wiped a spray of dirt off my face. "Ha. Got you!"

Elysian scuttled over. "Good work, kid. I think we did great today."

We? I rolled my eyes.

Elysian had spoken too soon. Or maybe he jinxed me, because the next moment, Daikan propelled himself upright with more power than I'd thought possible, sending me flying back through the air as he roared angrily.

"Ugh." Of all the places to land, it had to be in a pile of frozen dog poo. "Gross." *Why did I always have to land in something completely revolting?!*

I looked up just in time to see Elysian unleash an attack of his own. My dragon's bright celestial fire hit its mark as I stood up and hurriedly tried to clean myself up. Being a superhero is not as important as looking like one, in my opinion.

"Augh!" Daikan cried, the dragon fire slowly eating away at his colorful clothes and sizzling into his wrinkly skin. Even though I love my barbeque, it was a gruesome sight to watch him flap and burn. It probably would have been more enjoyable if he was dead. And plucked.

"Finish him!" Elysian called out.

"No one defeats me," I murmured, letting myself smile. *For once, we are going to get along all right without—*

284

A hot, blazing arrow of light suddenly soared out of nowhere. It struck the demonic creature in the head, unleashing a small bright explosion and bombing out brain residue. I jumped back and shielded my face. When I peeked over seconds later, Daikan was gone.

I groaned. I'd thought too soon. *She's here.*

Following the trajectory of the arrow, I looked up. And there she was.

Starry Knight, skillfully perched in the trees, was looking down on me, both literally and figuratively. "I told you to stay away from this business," she called out in a disdainful greeting, as was her per usual.

"Oh, just go away," I stomped my way over to my supposed counterpart. "I was doing just fine until you showed up. *And* I was here earlier than you."

"You are just getting in the way." She glared back, tightening her lips, obviously irritated. "It's clear you still don't know much about them, do you, *Wingdinger?*"

Since I was pretty sure she was making fun of me in addition to insulting me, I bit my bottom lip angrily, raging for blood. That was just like her, to disregard all the effort I'd espoused trying to learn more about the different demons suddenly plaguing our city. Believe me, between the *eelas*, the *bakreels,* and the *bakreels,* I'd had more than enough outer dimensional demon instruction.

But even so, who really cared if I didn't know that much yet? All I really knew for sure was that I had to fight them.

285

That had to count for a lot of it—over half of it, really. And the other stuff, well, I'd figure it out later, when I had the time and/or the inkling to care.

Starry Knight jumped down from the heights of the tree. "Since you appeared, I've had to save you more than I've had to defeat these monsters."

"Hey! I got some of them, too," I protested. *At least two or three, anyway … out of ten or twenty or … Who's really counting here anyway?* "I would've had this one, too, if you hadn't stolen my chance!"

"I'm sure you wouldn't have been able to do it," Starry Knight replied, waving me off. "You haven't gotten any stronger in the last weeks. Just give up and leave this to me. Oh, and I'd make sure to get some stain remover on your clothes." She flipped her long hair over her shoulder before she flew off, her stark white wings beating gracefully.

The embarrassment and anger burned, steaming hot. I thrust my fingers into my "wingdings" at the sides of my head, for which I was named, and tried not to scream. The pain of tearing at my feather-crown didn't help.

And neither did Elysian, of course. (He never does, trust me.)

"Don't worry about it, kid," Elysian told me. "You'll get the next one."

"What if I don't?" I asked sharply. "What then?"

"Don't do this to yourself. She's not worth it." Elysian

transformed. As a changeling dragon, he had the ability to transform into any reptile, but he often just pushed back his wings, sucked in his big dragon belly, and shrunk down to the size of a small lizard or chameleon. It was handy for travel purposes, I had to admit, but more often than not it meant he was nearby. And I didn't really like that.

"Maybe she's got a point. *She* seems to be getting more powerful." I doubted Elysian had noticed the increasing intensity of Starry Knight's arrows in the past few weeks. I also doubted he'd be able to refrain from making some irritating comment about it if I brought it up.

"Don't forget, we don't know much about her," Elysian said, honestly and exasperatedly. "If you really think she's getting more powerful, it could be a problem."

"You think?" I snorted distastefully. *Of course she is a problem! She'd been a problem since day one.* "How do you think she does it? How do you think I can get strong enough to beat her?"

"You're supposed to be concerned with the demons, so forget about her."

"You know what I mean."

"Frankly, I agree with Starry Knight; it's your own fault you're not getting more powerful."

"What?!" My gaze blazed into Elysian's, and he (wisely) shuffled back a few feet. "How can you say that? You're the one who's supposed to be 'mentoring me' or however you put it."

THE STARLIGHT CHRONICLES

"I cannot teach a know-it-all!" Elysian glared at me. "Look, you've accepted the task of defending the world from the Sinisters, but you're still as arrogant and self-centered as you always were. And it's worse since you've been given the powers. You still rely mostly on your guesswork to get the job done."

I motioned to my uniform, my transformed self. "Selfish? How can you say that? Do you know what I'd rather be doing while I'm fighting off the forces supposedly bent on destroying the world? I could be on a date!"

"Ugh! You make this so hard!" Elysian sighed. "You might have accepted the truth of your destiny, but there's more to believing than just accepting the truth. There's more to power than strength."

I muttered out a string of curses, probably a bit too loudly for Elysian's taste, because he chastised me a moment later. "You could get a lot more powerful if you just had some self-control."

"What do you mean by that?"

"I mean you can't even control your language, or your anger, or your actions. No wonder the demons laugh at you! You'll bring about your own destruction soon enough with that kind of attitude."

Before I could respond, the large clock tower in the city chimed, and I had another reason to hate my life. "Aw, great! It's after my curfew! Cheryl and Mark are going to be upset. Can tonight get any worse?"

Almost as soon as the words were out of my mouth, Elysian piped up with a half-smug, "Here comes the press."

And right on cue, a desperate-looking journalist hopped out of some nearby bushes, followed by several more of his camera-wielding posse. "Excuse me, Mr. Wingdinger, sir, can we get a couple of questions?"

I immediately ran for cover.

"Stop! We need to talk to you!"

"Come back, we want to make a deal! You'll be rich!"

"Where's Starry Knight?"

Anyone could tell you I was not usually shy in front of the camera. But the last thing I wanted was to do was to take financial responsibility for all the buildings and vehicles and other stuff that had been damaged in the previous months, and the blame for all of the people I hadn't saved. These were the major reasons I ran away from the press and cringed at the thought of interviews.

"Come on, Elysian," I said quietly. "Fly us away from these soul-suckers."

Elysian cocked an eyebrow at the irony and smothered a laugh, transforming once more. Moments later, we were safe and out of reach.

THE STARLIGHT CHRONICLES

How did this all happen? How did I manage to get drafted into humanity's last defense in an interdimensional war?

Truth be told, I wasn't exactly sure how it all began. All I really know was the day this mess exploded into my life, I'd been thinking about much more important matters. Much, much more important matters ...

AUTHOR'S ACKNOWLEDGEMENTS
EDITOR

Jennifer C. Sell

Jennifer Clark Sell is a professional book editor and proofreader. She works from her home in Southern California. With her years of professional and personal experience, she offers several quality packages for authors. Find her at

https://www.facebook.com/JenniferSellEditingService.

Photo Credit: Savannah Sell

AUTHOR'S ACKNOWLEDGEMENTS
COVER ILLUSTRATOR

Amalia Chitulescu

Amalia Iuliana Chitulescu is a digital artist from Campina, Romania. Raised in a small town, this self-taught artist has a technique which is delineated by the contrast between obscurity and enlightenment, using dark elements in a dreamy world. Her areas of expertise include the use of theatrical concepts to create a macabre and surrealistic world that still maintains a highly recognizable attachment to reality. Bridging a diaphanous environment with light elements, an eerie view, she creates a dream world of dark beauty, done with a blend of photography and digital painting. Find her at
https://www.facebook.com/Amalia.Chitulescu.Digital.Art

Photo Credit: Amalia Chitulescu

OTHER WORKS BY C. S. JOHNSON

The Starlight Chronicles
An Epic Fantasy Adventure Series

Slumbering (Book 1 of the Starlight Chronicles)

Awakening: A Christmas Episode of the Starlight Chronicles

Calling (Book 2 of the Starlight Chronicles)

Falling: A Starry Knight Episode of the Starlight Chronicles

Submerging (Book 3 of the Starlight Chronicles)

Seeing: A Wedding Episode of the Starlight Chronicles

Remembering (Book 4 of the Starlight Chronicles)

Belonging: A Date Night Episode of the Starlight Chronicles

Continuing (Book 5 of the Starlight Chronicles)

Reflecting: A Dream Episode of the Starlight Chronicles

Outpouring (Book 6 of the Starlight Chronicles)

Reawakening: A Rebirth Episode of the Starlight Chronicles

Everlasting (Book 7 of the Starlight Chronicles)

Searching (A Prequel to the Starlight Chronicles)

THE STARLIGHT CHRONICLES

THE STARLIGHT CHRONICLES

READY FOR BOOK 1?

Check out *Slumbering* online at your favorite ebook retailer! Thank you for reading! Please leave a review for this book and check out www.csjohnson.me for other books and updates!

298